To Joel,

with my

#galaxygirl

To infinity and beyond!

(or something like that ☺)

Praise for *#galaxygirl*

#galaxygirl

BEV SMITH

For Sophie, Amie and Chloe, with love.
And for all the Esmes in the world…

PLEASE HELP

Dear Reader,
If you come across this blog, please tell my mum about it. She doesn't 'do' the internet.
   She lives here:
                Miss Melanie Tickle,
                12 Daisy Way,
                Bournecombe,
                England,
                Planet Earth

Hi Mum,

So, I guess you've noticed I'm missing? You've probably asked my teachers and the kids at school where I am by now. Well, they're telling the truth, I'm not with them.
   You see the thing is, I'm actually in outer space. Don't panic though, I'm having a blast! It's AMAZING. They've got all kinds of exciting stuff going on up here, you'd love it.
   And gravity is completely overrated – in space no one sees you wobble.
   Brilliant. ☺
   So anyway, I was abducted by aliens. Although, I allowed myself to be abducted so, technically,

I ran away.

I honestly didn't expect to end up quite so far. I thought we were just going to see the moon, whizz around the stars and hang out for a bit, before heading back.

I'm on a planet called Kratos, Stella is here too. You were right about her, but she's not just a bit weird. She's an alien. She's one of the nicer ones though. She saved me from falling off the edge of a galactic crater yesterday, rocketing across from the other side in 0.22 nanoseconds. Sounds impossible, I know, but it's a piece of cake for her. And not just any old cake either – but the kind of cake that has glittery fancy icing with cream doodles, topped off with those sprinkly bits. The kind that stands out from the cake crowd. Like the ones Gran used to make...

I miss you much more than I thought I would, but I don't miss your boyfriends. Especially the latest one. To be honest, most of the stuff which used to upset me doesn't seem so important now that I'm millions and billions of light years away from home.

I'm still biting my nails, but the good news is they grow back much quicker here in outer space.

Stella said I should find a way to tell you about everything that's happened, to help you 'come to terms' with my departure. I'll tell you the whole story right from the start, so keep coming back to my blog.

Love you round the world and back again.

Esme

#galaxygirl

x

1

9 January

Earth to Esme

It was the antenna that first caught my attention. As she walked across the quad it sprouted casually from under her hat, like it was checking the school out. I should've guessed something weird was going on when Mrs Snotgrass pulled her aside and repositioned it, rather than tell her off for not being in the *approved* uniform. They were whispering, the cold heating up their breath, releasing tiny pockets of gas into the morning air.

Every atom in my body tensed as they turned to look at me. *Oh no, she's going to ask me again.*

As Snottypants and the newbie walked towards me I clocked The Populars, clustered together at ten-to-two. Becky Morgan and her cronies were leaning against the windows of the art corridor, lazily watching my predicament. As ever, they looked like they could freeze a puddle of mercury with a single glance, such was the level of their cool.

Next to them stood Dylan Grant, aka Delicious Dylan – *just in case you're wondering, that means,* '*also known as*'. My stomach did the usual cartwheels, somersaults and double back-flips whenever I saw him. Leaving me completely 'in-compost-mentis', as Gran used to say.

Or something like that.

'Earth to Esme. Are you with us?' asked Snottypants, pointing her long, supernova nose in my direction. Her hair dangling like a bunch of sweaty cheese-strings, all jostling for space on her head.

'Er… what? Yes… Yes, of course,' I stuttered, dragging my eyes away from Delicious Dylan and back to the near future. *Blimey, this girl looks even weirder close up. No competition for Delicious Dylan here!*

'Esme, I'd like you to look after our new girl.'

Well isn't that just double PE on a wet Monday morning terrific! I get to look after the weirdo in fancy dress for the day.

'Meet Stella. She has specifically asked for you to show her all aspects of the school. I trust this is acceptable to you?' Not waiting for an answer she turned to face the newbie again. 'Esme is an excellent example of a Year 8 student. Learn as much from her as possible about human girls within this age group.'

'Now, please provide Stella with a quick tour around the school,' she ordered. 'I will take great pleasure in meeting up with you both later.' With that she tottered off across the icy quad on her high heels, no doubt looking for some other poor, unsuspecting student to harass.

Why do ALL teachers think:

10

a) *They know everything about you?*

b) *They can boss you around?*

c) *They don't need to ask for your opinion when dishing out stuff to do?*

d) They're always right?

I looked back at Stella, who was grinning widely from ear to ear, somewhat disconcertingly 2.54 centimetres from my face.

'Greetings,' she declared, interrupting the silence. 'I am exceedingly eager to learn about your school. I understand your reluctance to show me around, but we are going to become close acquaintances.'

At this point I was even more concerned. This girl sounded like she'd been to a posh school, swallowed several posh dictionaries and was chucking them all back up.

'O-K-A-a-a-y,' I said, eyes focused on the ground. After a long and awkward pause I put on a brave face, accepted my mission and decided to accomplish it as best I could.

'So, Markham High isn't special, quite the opposite in fact. We aren't a talented bunch, unless you rate the less-than-useful skills of texting, snogging, lesson-wrecking and bullying. It's a massive place, but you'll soon get used to it.' I shrugged. 'Come on, we've got eleven minutes until registration.

'Teachers here can be tricky. Miss Day teaches history. She's getting a bit past it now – everyone thinks she'll leave this year. Personally, I think she should've gone years ago. Mrs Snotgrass is new here, she's really weird. Loads of teachers have left since she arrived. I–'

'Affirmative. My file contains this information, but I require information about the students. Especially you. Tell me about your mother.'

File? This girl was freaking me out now. And she seemed genuinely interested in me.

Random.

*

That afternoon, I walked home from school with all the enthusiasm of an asthmatic tortoise who'd developed a painful limp. I wondered what new delights awaited at that place we optimistically called 'home'.

Isaac and Maisie have perfected the art of being the most annoying little brother and sister in the world. I had no doubt they'd be applying these skills when I got in. Especially as *their* dad was taking them out for the evening – which always made them more irritating than usual.

I wondered, not for the first time, what *my* dad was like… You never liked to talk about him, Mum, but whatever happened between the two of you shouldn't have stopped me having a relationship with him.

Something I read in the RE classroom came to mind – *If life chucks lemons at you, just pick them up and make lemonade.* Right then, I felt like I had enough lemons to set up a lemonade factory *AND* a chain of lemonade shops across the country.

Daisy Way was as busy as ever. Kids playing football in the street, being shouted at by the old man at number forty-four. Two dustbins had already been knocked over, so I didn't blame him.

The street's name was a clever disguise, designed to trick people into thinking it was a lovely place to live. But the noisiest people in Bournecombe all seem to have been dumped here.

As usual there was plenty going on when I walked in. You were with your mates in the front room, the TV properly blaring out. One of them was in full flow, sobbing about the latest 'chapter' in her love life.

One of your friend's kids was crying to Maisie about hurting his toe, 'the one which went to market'. Her other kid was busy stealing marbles from Maisie's jar, the one she got for her seventh birthday.

Isaac was on the toilet, shouting, 'Hey everybody, my poo is ready and waiting to leave bottom town, right about... *NOW! Choo choo! Choo choo!*'

Situation normal.

While you were busy ignoring all of this, I wandered into the kitchen. I couldn't help overhear you trying to comfort your friend. 'Never mind, there's plenty more fish in the sea.' You said the same thing to her when she broke up with her last boyfriend.

I honestly don't know why you bother. Maybe you should all just focus on your daytime TV shows and forget about men?

With *Come Whine With Me* blaring out from the front room, I managed to find a clean glass amongst the debris of the kitchen cupboards. Taking my juice upstairs and lying down on my bed I thought how, just for once, I'd like to come home to a quiet house. Not have two or three of your mates moping about the place.

In my fantasy the house would be tidy, there would be dinner cooking, homemade cakes fresh out of the oven, no TV screaming out.

You would welcome me home with a big smile on your face and show some interest in how my day at school had gone. You'd ask what homework I had, then offer to help me—

Actually, scrap the bit about the homework! I didn't want you *THAT* involved. It would mean having you on my case and having to actually do the stuff …

Before I knew it, I was raiding my secret stash of biscuits and sweets, munching my way to certain, if temporary, happiness. Little did I know my life was about to get busy. Not to mention exciting, in an 'oops I've been voluntarily abducted by aliens and been taken to a far-off planet' kind of way.

Gotta go now, but stay tuned for more.

Peace out, brussel sprout. ☺

Esme

x

2

10 January

That food really suits you

I remember the first time I ever heard about aliens. We were watching a documentary with your ex, Gary – the one from Grimsville, who used to spend all day watching TV in his underpants. Anyway, the programme was about some place in America where an alien had been found. He told me he'd been abducted by aliens when he was twelve.

This, coming from the man who believed the Earth was flat and dinosaurs helped to build the pyramids… I couldn't think for the life of me why, of all the people on Earth, anyone would choose to abduct *him*. That alone convinced me aliens didn't exist.

How wrong can you be?

The week I left there was a ton of reports on the news about 'strange sightings' in the skies over Bournecombe. At first, I didn't take any notice of the usual crazies on TV, but the more time I spent around Stella, the more I realised there was definitely something out there.

It wasn't just the weird antennae on her head – a feature, I should add, nobody else seemed to notice – but other things. Like, how she shoved a tissue in my hand before I'd even sneezed, not to mention the speed at which she rocketed across the dining hall when the food was laid out. Nobody's that hungry, right?

Stella's second day at school was eventful. For both of us. I was stuck with her again, courtesy of Snottypants, but managed to escape after tutor time.

My first lesson was with Mrs Harrison for double maths – the teacher whose only claim to fame was the furry undergrowth nestling under her chin. Out of all of the teachers you never met, Mum, this one was the worst. I took a deep breath and gingerly opened the door to Harrison's lair.

As I crept in I felt like that guy on TV, the one who does the nature programmes, David wotsisface. The one with that deep, breathy voice…

So here we are, entering into the natural habitat of the greater-crested human – Hairius Maximus, or as it is more commonly known, The Hairy Teacher. We must be careful not to alert the creature to our presence, for Hairius Maximus attacks can be as unpredictable as they are unprovoked.

My internal commentary playing, I crept across the room to my chair, trying not to be noticed by Hairy Harrison, who was busy tidying her desk.

If we can just get to the safety of a chair then we'll be able to observe this fascinating creature in its natural, if hostile habitat – the classroom.

I went to sit down when there was a swift breeze, a flash of colour and… I was on Stella's lap! Somehow she'd got to my chair before me. Everybody noticed, the loud laughter being a sure sign. Even the chair seemed to find it amusing.

'Esme Tickle, what do you think you're doing?' Harrison's voice rumbled across the room, like a Mexican wave, building in a crescendo until it hit my ears like a thunder clap. 'I'm sure the new girl doesn't appreciate you jumping on her. Sit on your own chair. *Immediately!*'

Oh.

My.

Days.

The shame. As if it wasn't enough that everyone called me 'Ginger Nut' and 'Tango', now I'd get teased about this too. ☹

At the end of the lesson Stella followed me, and of course I had no choice but to hang out with her. I headed for the dining hall trying to ignore her but, fortunately for me, she didn't seem to notice my rudeness.

'What's a no-life like you doing in a place like this, then? This is our table. Now move, Ginger Nut.' The noise and bustle died down as everyone turned to watch the action. Becky Morgan, aka Mean Girl extraordinaire, with her crew. The girl who couldn't slither past me without hissing something.

I opened my mouth to speak but Stella cut in, 'I did not comprehend you had offensive people existing here too.' She looked across at Becky. 'It is you who must depart! Harassing us should be of insignificant concern for you.'

Stella caught my eye, then, almost imperceptibly, flicked her eyes over Becky and her crew. Each of the girls' trays upended over them. The whole dining hall, which had stopped to witness my humiliation, was now in hysterics.

'Hey, that food really suits you, Becky,' someone shouted. Suddenly Stella didn't seem such a pain to have around.

With the attention off of us we went outside. Finding an empty bench at the side of the school field, we sat down. An oak tree crouched over us, as if it was trying to listen in on our conversation.

'What just happened in there?' I asked.

'It is most straightforward – events occur when I concentrate them into existence,' she said, as if it was the most natural thing in the world.

'*Whaaaat* are you talking about?'

'I am gifted with this ability. It has ensured my popularity amongst the teachers at my school. Members of the teaching staff at the educational establishment I attend hold me in great esteem,' she said. 'Sadly, my peers do not esteem me highly.'

'Blimey, I wish I'd met you sooner, just think of the fun we could've had!'

'This is not a great concern. As I have previously indicated, we are going to become close acquaintances. So much so that it is inevitable I should communicate crucial information about myself.' She lowered her voice, glancing to the left and right. 'I am a student from the Planet Kratos, visiting Earth on the STAR Programme.'

'Run that by me again?' I gave her my best *I don't have a clue what you're talking about* look.

'I will duplicate my sentence for you. You must pay great heed to my statements. It is of the utmost importance that confidentiality is maintained,' she whispered, looking around again, before moving closer. 'My natural habitat is not Planet Earth. Rather, I come from Kratos, a planet which is 600 billion light years away. For my student project I have joined the Species Tourism and Restoration Programme on this trip to your planet.'

'So what you're basically saying is that you're an alien?' I whispered.

'Affirmative. However, on my planet *you* are the alien. Nevertheless,' she conceded, 'I accept that, from your Earthling perspective, I am an alien.'

'You don't look like an alien.'

'You have encountered an alien previous to our acquaintance?'

I shook my head.

'This was my precise judgement. Therefore, your position for identifying the features of an alien is ineffective.'

'Well, there's no need to be rude.'

'I apologise profusely. I am finding my experience on your planet to be exceedingly overwhelming,' she said softly. 'The STAR Programme has special technology which provides us with a human disguise.

I *do* have an altered appearance when on Kratos.'

'Well you didn't disguise your antennae very well!'

'Affirmative. Fortunately Mrs Snotgrass concealed it, before others became aware of it.'

'Haha, don't tell me she's an alien too? That'd explain a lot!' I laughed, then stopped as I caught the look on her face. 'What? You mean she *is* an alien? You're kidding me! How many more are there around here?'

'There are merely two others currently in Bournecombe. However, there are additional Kratons in the South of England. They are gathering items to take home for research.'

As I sat deep in thought, wondering how many other teachers could possibly be aliens, I spotted Delicious Dylan. He was walking across the quad, all floppy brown hair and skateboard. He saw me and waved. I couldn't stop myself. 'Can you, erm... "concentrate" Dylan Grant into being my boyfriend?'

'No, my gift does not permit me to influence people, merely material substances.'

Shrugging off my disappointment we made plans to meet up after school. That was the afternoon I brought her home to meet you, Mum.

I was so pleased to have found someone to hang out with, even if she was weirder than anyone I'd ever met.

Gotta dash now.

Hot to trot, jelly tot. ☺

Esme

x

3

☆

16 January

☆ ## Save the snails and animals and other stuff

☆

I do miss you but I wouldn't have left if it wasn't for you and your latest boyfriend. Since when did you care about animal rights? I mean, protesting with him about the new road in town is one thing, but to do it outside my school took it to a whole new level of cringe.

In.

Front.

Of.

Everyone.

It's completely beyond me why you would think holding some kind of ridiculous protest was a good way to solve *anything.* All anyone ever does is make a nuisance of themselves, shouting and wailing.

It wouldn't have been quite so bad if you hadn't been waving a stupid placard around with 'save the snails and other animals and stuff wot might be livin 'ere' written on it. Everyone knew you were my mum – which obviously I tried to deny – and took

21

the mickey out of me even more.

Then you broke into the school, wrecking the science project we were working on. Just because we were dissecting frogs. I'd been paired up with Delicious Dylan too. Our work was completely destroyed!

Of course the headteacher went on and on about it in assembly, not taking her eyes off me once. I wanted the ground to open up and swallow me whole.

When I got home from school I was gutted, and you didn't even notice. I walked into the house expecting you to at least make some kind of apology, but you were in the kitchen laughing with The Boyfriend.

'Anything we can help you with, love?' he asked, like *I* was the one visiting.

'Mum, do you have any idea what you've done today?' I asked, not even looking at him.

'Yes, darlin', I… I mean… we've made a stand for all the creatures of the world that can't stand up for themselves. 'aven't we, poppet?' you said, curling your arm around the waist of the latest intruder, smiling up at him dreamily.

'We certainly made a point. I'm sure they'll not be forgetting yer good self or me, Pete Wazzock, for quite some time.' he said, smirking as he tugged you closer, the veins in his skinny arms bulging,

'You've made a stand for some weird and highly unattractive species of snail, which *nobody* – apart from French cooks – has shown *any* interest in over the previous six millennia.' I felt my face get redder and redder. 'And as for the frogs… that was a project I was working on with the most amazing boy in school. Everyone knows it was you! You've ruined everything!'

'Ooh, Esme's got a boyfriend!' I wanted to curl up with embarrassment all over again. 'Hey, Maisie, Isaac, Esme's got a boyfriend.'

They came scurrying in, dancing around me. Two blonde jumping beans, chanting, 'Esme's got a boyfriend, Esme's got a boyfriend.'

You were so wrapped up in Protest Pete that you didn't notice how upset I was.

I'd arranged to meet Stella in the park before tea, which was just as well because it felt like nobody in this family has cared about me since Gran died. I used to love escaping to her flat, knowing she'd always listen to me. What I wouldn't have given to spend one more hour with her…

Stella and me had spent so much time together since we'd met it felt like she understood me more than anyone. She knew about what you'd done in school and had heard some of the kids teasing me, so she got it. Alien or not, I don't think I've ever had such a good friend.

'I can't take it any more,' I said, plonking down on the grass. '*That* man is in the house and is treating it like his own. I've only ever met him once before, and that was in the off-licence at the bottom of our street. He's at my place *right* now ordering Maisie and Isaac around like they're *his* kids.'

'Communicate to me, Esme, has your mother

provided any indication that she comprehends your current emotional condition?'

'No. That's the point. She doesn't get it at all, and it seems like she doesn't care. She's putting this idiot bloke before her kids.' I pulled up a handful of grass and threw it down again.

'She is evidently an individual with a profound requirement for companionship. Her judgement appears to be imprecise in this area. On Kratos we do not permit our children to be treated in such an abysmal manner.' She gave me a sideways glance.

'What's it like living there?'

'It is exceedingly magnificent. We have the most organised society. Incredible scenery. Advanced technology. And my parents are sincerely the most agreeable individuals you could ever desire to become acquainted with,' she said. 'If you ever visited you would have complete comprehension, of this I am certain.'

'You're so lucky being able to travel so much. I haven't even been on a plane.'

'Affirmative. I have a deep appreciation of my privilege. Technology is developing so rapidly on Kratos that children have opportunities our parents only considered within their dreams. I am in excessive anticipation of my return.'

'I wish I could— *wait*, what do you mean, your return? We're just getting to know each other!'

'My departure must commence within the following five hours.'

'I don't want you to go, Stella, you're the best

thing around here.'

'This is not an appropriate environment for my health. I am only enabled to maintain a perfect state of health for a certain period of time. However I am informed that my current phase on this planet must be terminated today.'

'What will I do? Who will I talk to? No one else cares like you do.' I cried then, the grass pulling having lost its therapeutic effect.

'Having pondered this dilemma I've contemplated a solution which might be of mutual benefit.' I glanced up at her quickly, not sure what she had in mind, but grateful she was at least considering me in all of this.

'I would consider it an honour if you would contemplate accompanying me to Kratos.'

'*Whaaaaaat?* Are you crazy? My mum would never let me go!'

'It appears her focus is elsewhere. Perhaps she is content to permit you to construct your own decisions?' she asked, looking at me intensely. 'Perhaps you should abstain from communicating with your mother regarding this matter?'

'Are you serious? You mean, actually leave my mum, sister, brother, school and Planet Earth? And not tell them?'

'Affirmative. You will not grieve for any of these. Your deep unhappiness is apparent whenever we converse. Departing with me will enhance your life experience, of this I am assured.'

I'm not going to lie, it didn't take much to persuade

me. Especially when she put it like that.

What did I have to lose?

Better whizz, sherbert fizz. ☺

Esme

x

4

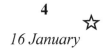

16 January

Remain inaudible

I arranged to meet Stella at the bottom of Barrow Hill at 9 p.m. It was an especially clear night – I remember, because there were so many stars. Normally I don't notice these things but, on this night, I was hyper-vigilant seeing as I was about to go up there.

I'd forgotten how far it was, but luckily I'd remembered to bring a bag full of chocolate to keep me company. There were some strange, tiny pink lights in the sky, twinkling like a mini-disco was going on. The trees looked properly creepy, like they were trying to hide something sinister. But those lights were mesmerising.

By the time I'd walked 987 steps I saw her. Excited, I ran the last stretch. 'Phew,' I said, out of breath, 'I was worried you might have changed your mind and gone without me!'

'Never would this occur in a million light years,' she said, grinning at me in a way which had become much less annoying now.

'How will I *actually* get on board the spaceship?'

'Simple, you observe my actions, then duplicate them. You must refrain from anxiety. You will witness an unexpected event. All will be satisfactory once we land on Kratos, where reconfiguration occurs and our bodies are returned to normal.'

'Returned to normal? What's the *not* normal part before we get 'returned to normal'?'

It was at this point I started to get cold feet. I wasn't sure I'd be able to go through with it.

'Do not fear, for FEAR is merely False Expectations Appearing Real.'

'Haha, you've been reading the posters in the RE classroom.' She'd stopped me worrying in an instant, but not in the way she'd intended.

'Affirmative. I have acquired a book for my mother to read – *The Gigantic Book of Inspirational But Ridiculously Cheesy Quotes*. It will become a favourite of hers,' she said, setting off for the woods behind the hill.

We walked through the woods for some time. I had to hold onto her to stop myself from tripping over the logs and branches scattered across the ground. It was hard work keeping up the same pace.

Eventually we came to a clearing. In the middle sat a toy spaceship. It was silver, 43.4cm wide, 25.3cm tall, with pink laser lights beaming from each section. I was about to run over to pick it up, when Stella grabbed my arm and pulled me back under the cover of the trees.

'Ow,' I said, wincing as one of the branches clawed at me.

'Remain concealed,' she whispered.

'Why are we hiding?' I asked, rubbing my arm.

'Prior to our arrival on Kratos, you must remain obscured from the others. This is our spaceship.' She pointed at the toy in the clearing.

'*Whaaat?!* You can't be serious?'

'Affirmative. It has come to gather me and two other students, who will be present imminently. This is the designated hour of our collection.'

'How in heaven's name are we going to fit into that?'

'Simply observe, and all will be clarified. Soon others will commence arrival.'

Three minutes and eleven seconds later, I was still waiting, not to mention struggling to stop myself from sneezing. It doesn't sound like a long time, but when you're trying not to alert a bunch of aliens to your hiding place *and* attempting to avoid getting zapped into oblivion it feels like forever.

In the end it couldn't be stopped and, having no choice but to turn in her direction, I did the unthinkable and sneezed in Stella's face.

'I'm so sorry,' I whispered. 'I tried really hard to stop it, but my sneeze just wanted to come out and party.'

'Do not consider this a cause for great concern.' She wiped her face with a sleeve. 'Observe, they have arrived.' I followed the direction of her finger and saw two figures appear on the opposite side of the clearing.

'Hang on a minute, that looks like Tom and Calen

from Year 11! Don't tell me they're aliens too?'

She winked at me, then carried on staring.

That explains why they've been acting so weird. Sitting on the school field at lunch and break, staring at the hedges and grass. Even in the pouring rain.

'It is Obi 17,608, alongside his fellow student Darth 21,012,' she whispered. 'Obi is the student with the maximum grades for technology at my school. We all arrived at the identical moment together. Their mission was to select and bring to Kratos six species of plants, along with a tree which is highly admired by my people.'

'Looks like they got what they came for.' They dragged the tree across the ground, finally coming to a standstill in the middle of the clearing.

'Of notable interest to us is your eggplant. We wish to grow them to ensure that Kratos has a permanent supply, in the event that our birds cease production.'

'Stella, you do know you only get eggs from birds, don't you? *No* eggplant is going to give you *any* eggs.' I rolled my eyes in dismay. 'And that's what Americans call them – we call them aubergines in England. I thought your people were way more advanced than us lot?'

I'm not sure if she heard me, or if she was ignoring me – she kept her eyes fixed on Obi.

'Our scientists are currently engaged in creating a device which will enable us to transport exhibits back from Earth, via a much less complicated procedure,' she whispered. 'Soon we will be able to return to Kratos extracting up to a hundred items – including animals – at a time.'

'As long as you don't take too many, I mean some of our species are disappearing.' I was surprised to hear myself defending them.

We spent the next one minute, seven seconds in silence.

'Why have the boys got numbers after their name?'

'On Kratos we are not given a surname unless in a position of seniority. After we receive our birth name, we receive a number which informs us of the number of people who have been assigned the name since we commenced creating records.' She sounded so proud as she was telling me this. 'So, Obi is the 17,608th person to be given his birth name. Mine is 12,614. You will be Esme 1. Nobody has ever taken this name on Kratos.'

'Brilliant.' I liked the sound of this more and more.

'You must remain inaudible. Be vigilant, observe closely.' She motioned towards the spaceship. A slightly larger, single pink light began to flash, with gaps of 0.89 seconds between each flicker.

Obi and Darth crept towards the tiny alien craft, dragging the tree and plants behind them. The closer they got, the smaller they became. They literally shrank before my eyes. By the time they'd got to the spaceship they were tiny enough to fit on the steps and go through the door.

Amazing.

Stella placed her finger under my jaw – which had pretty much landed on my chest – and pushed it up. *What have I just seen? Surely I'm not going to go through the exact same process???*

'You will experience the exact same process,' she said. 'Linger until I am beyond the door, then it is essential you hasten to follow me. The craft will delay for two minutes before the door is secured. I will prepare a confidential place equipped for you to remain concealed.'

'Stella, what was your mission?' It occurred to me that she wasn't carrying anything to take back.

She turned to me, hesitating, 'I must depart, dialogue will occur during a future occasion.' She walked to the spaceship. Like the others, she gradually shrunk as she got closer.

There was nothing for it. I'd come this far so I sure as heck wasn't going back. She'd insisted I'd be fine, so I decided to trust her. Having seen her disappear, I crept out of my hiding place behind the tree, creeping towards the spaceship. Like the others, I began to shrink the closer I got, every molecule in my body twitching and tingling. By the time I reached the steps my body was the right size to fit inside.

I raced up the stairs, and managed to get in just before the doors shut. She was inside waiting for me, and hurried me into a special chamber.

It was perfect, having all the essentials a traveller could need:

A chair.

A cushion.

A blanket.

Oxygen.

I settled down and waited for lift off.

Soon the whole craft was shaking from side to side. I figured either one of the aliens had just done a mega-fart or we were taking off.

Whichever it was, I was a proper bag of nerves – it's not every day you get to take a journey into outer space.

Peachy keen, jelly bean. ☺

Esme

x

5

☆

16 January

☆ **Not in front of the children, dear**

☆ ☆

I expect you're thinking the journey here must have been really long? Well, because of their spectacular spaceships, the journey only took seven minutes, seventeen seconds. It was almost like we'd taken off and then… boom! We arrived!

Aided by my perfect stash of snacks, I survived in one piece. My face and body moved in all kinds of squishy directions though, and nothing seemed to be where it normally was.

At one point, I thought my Galaxy bars were going to jump out of the capsule, but luckily the only place they moved to was my mouth. It was funny, although I'm glad nobody else got to see it. I probably looked a lot like you after a night out on the town with your mates, Mum.

Messy. ☹

I could tell we'd arrived because the spaceship had stopped moving – always a dead giveaway. As I shifted to get more comfortable, wondering what would happen next, someone rapped on the capsule's roof.

'Are you experiencing good feelings, Esme?' Phew, it was just Stella.

'Yes, I'm fine. What happens now?' I could hear some shuffling then muttering. Had I been rumbled?

Then some more shuffling.

'We've obtained an oxygen suit for you to employ.'

'OK, thanks, wher—' I stopped. 'What do you mean *we*?!'

'The captain observed me returning to this spot and demanded to understand the purpose,' she said. 'My options were limited. I confessed and the captain wishes to converse with you. Please position this suit and helmet on your body, then you will find that respiration will be highly efficient for you.'

She opened a hatch in the door, and placed a package into the drop box. Once she'd safely shut the hatch I opened it my side. Inside was a shiny purple spacesuit, complete with a giant bubble of a helmet.

Shuffling around on my bum while tugging the suit on, I couldn't help being nervous about the near future. So many questions were going through my mind:

Will they lock me up?

Will they make me go home?

What is Kratos going to be like?

Will these aliens like me?

And, more importantly, will this suit make me look like a giant blueberry?

I stepped out of the capsule into a techie's dream

of a room, and was met by two pairs of eyes. Both sets of which belonged to the neon-green captain. He appeared to be in as much shock as me, barely speaking, making some kind of babbling noise. It sounded like a cross between a cat being tickled and a waterfall.

While his right eyes were looking at Stella, his left ones were looking at me and his six green arms were waving around furiously, like a bunch of overexcited snakes at an end-of-year reptilian disco.

Six arms. Useful, I guess, if you're getting ready in the morning or if you've got an itchy bum, nose and foot at the same time.

The babbling, I later found out, was actually their native language.

Weird.

Weirder still was listening to Stella use it too. Not to mention the extra pair of eyes she'd grown, the six arms, the beautiful shade of green skin and long pink hair. Oh, and before I forget to mention it, she was now twice the size of me!

Eventually Stella turned back to face me. 'He requests that you depart alongside him. Nevertheless I have convinced him to permit you to set forth with my family. He has prior to this moment conversed with my father, who has authorised a visit from the Social Care Keepers.'

I didn't care who came to see me, I just wanted to find somewhere friendlier and less spaceshippy to hang out.

'Er... goodbye,' said the captain as I was leaving

the spaceship. 'I hope Kratos your stay enjoy on you.'

'Goodbye and thank you,' I offered, baffled by the jumble of words he had just thrown at me.

'All Kratons speak English. We become skilled promptly during our education,' she explained as we walked along a narrow corridor. 'The captain has problematic syntax. As does his daughter, Mars 15,122, whose acquaintance you will undoubtedly make.'

'Well at least he was friendly. I thought he'd blow a fuse after he found out I'd stowed away on his precious spaceship. Why wasn't he angry?'

'We may perhaps explore this dilemma on a later occasion,' she said, keeping her eyes fixed ahead. 'For now you must remain in confinement while our medical professionals ascertain the absence of germs from Earth.'

The team came in to check me over, taking forever. They kept staring goggle-eyed at me like they'd never seen a human before – which, of course, they hadn't.

They took my temperature, removed some blood for testing, then poked around in my ears and mouth. It was worse than the time Gran took me to hospital when I went down with food poisoning.

I was just beginning to question my decision to stowaway when the doctors gave me the all-clear. You'll be pleased to know that I don't have a cold or any other kind of bug, so they gave me permission to stay.

Stella brought her family in to meet me. It's funny,

because I never considered green to be good skin tone, but it's actually quite lovely. If you met them I'm sure you'd agree.

Her dad is called Armstrong 6,209. He's named after Neil, the first man on our moon. They know about our space exploration, by the way. They follow a lot of what we do. He has purple hair, which is tied in a ponytail, kind of reminds me of Protest Pete. Ugh...

Her mum is called Luna 58,003. She's gorgeous, aside from the three strands of hair hovering on her chin, which I did my best not to stare at. She has the most beautiful long hair, cascading down her back, right to her knees. The fact that it's blue is neither here nor there.

'Observe, I have transported a gift for you, Mother,' said Stella, handing over *The Gigantic Book of Inspirational But Ridiculously Cheesy Quotes*.

'This is delightful, so unexpected, you really are a thoughtful girl,' said Luna, opening the book briefly before putting it into her bag. 'I'll read it later, I want to spend time with you girls first.'

The family Jetcar revved up quickly as we left the spaceport, whizzing across the city's cola-coloured sky. There were literally hundreds of Jetcars, all going at the same speed, zigzagging and criss-crossing each other. I don't think you'd like to take your driving test up here, Mum.

'What's this place called?' I asked, staring out of the window in wonder.

'Perihelion,' replied Armstrong. 'It's the only

habitable city left on Kratos. Everyone lives here.'

'Everyone who's worth knowing,' said Luna. 'It's stunning, isn't it?' She turned to me, smiling.

The city stretched for miles and miles, with skyscrapers of all shapes and sizes. I was like a greedy kid, gobbling up the sights like sweeties. Armstrong moved the Jetcar closer to the ground so I could get a better look.

Below, thousands of people floated just above the ground on Hoverpacks. They were moving in and around the brightly coloured buildings.

The closer we got the noisier it became. By the time we were 6.4 metres above the ground, I needed earplugs to shield my ears from the noise of the Hoverpacks zooming along, swerving under and around the hundreds of animated advertising billboards.

'Do we have Hoverpacks?' I asked hopefully.

'Negative, my father refrains from permitting them.'

'Yes, they are too dangerous. You girls will be transported everywhere by Jetcar or maxi-taxi,' said Armstrong.

The locals were of the pea soup variety, so many different shades of green. Every time they passed each other they made an upside down 'V' sign with their index and middle finger. Apparently it's considered rude not to.

'The red buildings are state-owned,' said Armstrong, breaking and entering into my thoughts. 'The green ones belong to our religious orders.

Many people choose to follow the state religion here, but we are not forced to. Our purple buildings are commercial – within them you will find any product you could wish for. We will take you shopping soon.'

He curved the car around the side of a blue building – belonging to Kratos Broadcasting Corporation – before hovering over a green space. In the middle was a large body of water in the shape of a star. The lights surrounding it twinkled brightly on the water. Upon it were a number of square-shaped rowing boats, aliens paddling furiously to stay afloat.

'Can you see the building to your left, the one in the middle with the tallest spire?' asked Luna. I nodded. 'It's our government building. It's made of titanium, in fact all our buildings are. They need to be strong enough to endure our fierce winter. During Qoolt Kratos experiences awful storms. Stones and rocks fall from the sky, it can be very dangerous.'

It made winter in Bournecombe sound like a glorious summer day.

'Will we be able to visit the area over there?' I asked, pointing towards a vast open space on the edge of the city.

'Esme, that area is dangerous,' said Armstrong, frowning. 'It's called the Outlands, a barren environment, similar to the deserts on Earth. It will not be on our itinerary.'

'He is right. It's also the place where the Bad Ones live. Anyone who has committed a serious crime is sent there, banished forever from Perihelion by the Justice Keepers,' added Luna, staring into the distance. 'There have been generations of Armstrong's family who have been Justice Keepers. So we are especially keen to avoid this area.'

'Yes, there was an attempt made to kidnap my father ten years ago, led by notorious criminals who my father dispatched there,' said Armstrong. 'It made headline news. And broke my father. He never recovered and sadly passed across two years later.'

'So you have newspapers? TV? That's so random, I didn't expect you to have any of those things,' I said, trying to change the subject.

'Kratos and Earth have many similarities, but I think you will find Kratos' landscape very different to Earth's,' said Armstrong. 'Bordering the Outlands are the Floating Hills, a cluster of small mountains which contain a unique microclimate, causing them to float above a sea of frozen nitrogen. There is nowhere in the entire universe like it!'

'Wow, can we go?' I asked.

'No, it won't be possible. I was merely informing you, not suggesting a visit,' he said, tapping the steering wheel nervously. I was starting to feel like I'd have even less freedom up here than on Earth.

Stella looked like she was about to say something, but Luna shot her a look that would've stopped Isaac in his tracks. The atmosphere outside might've been thick, but even the strongest cake knife wouldn't have sliced through the atmosphere *inside* the car.

'There has been much discussion about a school trip to the Floating Hills,' said Stella, deciding to ignore her mum. 'It would be most beneficial to visit as it is the only habitat of the Greater Spotted Froid, Father.'

'What is *that* when it's at home?' I asked.

'It's a rare species which is only able to survive on the Floating Hills,' said Luna.

'It is remarkably similar to your frogs on Earth, but considerably reduced in dimension,' chipped in Stella.

'I do not wish to discuss this right now,' said Armstrong, before swerving to avoid an oncoming vehicle, throwing me across Stella. *'Shooting stars! Stay on your own side of the Jetpath!'* he shouted, before putting the brakes on, causing the car to jolt.

'Not in front of the children, dear,' said Luna, her eyebrows raised. 'We're perfectly safe, no harm done.'

'My father experiences Jetpath rage when he contemplates the inconsiderate nature of other drivers,' Stella whispered. 'Mother hates it when he uses that language, but you must not be fearful. His emotions will rapidly become reasonable.'

Didn't sound that bad to me. She should hear what your last boyfriend used to say, Mum. She'd probably keel over in shock.

'Why is your English so different to your mum and dad's?' I asked, hoping not to offend her.

'My English tutor was highly precise with your language. He learned to communicate through a dictionary which he acquired on a mission to Earth. This is the technique demonstrated to me in my early years. It is my preference to maintain it.'

I was right, she *had* swallowed a dictionary, metaphorically speaking.

*

I came at the right time. It's Alsun at the moment, and the suns – *they've got three, can you believe it?* – stay out for sixteen hours a day. Shame I can't sunbathe though. Despite the triple dose of solar rays, it's really cold.

Also, if I take my suit off I'll float up into the sky and never be seen again. Oh, and I'll stop breathing. I prefer to stay grounded, not to mention alive.

They've been so welcoming, I can't tell you how wonderful it feels to be part of a proper family, with a mum and dad. Like some of the other kids at Markham High. Sorry if that makes you feel bad, but it's what I've always wanted.

Gotta dance, smarty pants. ☺

Esme

   x

6

☆

16–17 January

☆ **The maximum official**

person

☆

☆

Stella's house is ginormous. It stands head and shoulders above the rest of the street. It's five storeys high, with four spires, each topped with a huge satellite dish. They're seriously addicted to TV here.

The street is full of different types of houses. Some small. Some big. Some round. Some square. They don't really have proper gardens – just grey, dusty patches of land with a few rocks. The street was even more uninviting than Daisy Way, at least we have colour.

When we finally arrived at Stella's house there were tons of reporters from the press on the doorstep.

'How on Kratos did they find out?' asked Armstrong. 'She's only been here a couple of hours!'

'Who are they waiting for?' I asked. At which they turned and stared at me, a look of disbelief on their faces. 'What? Why are you looking at me like that?'

'I am convinced that you are jesting,' said Stella. 'They are lingering close to the façade of our

44

residence in anticipation of your arrival.'

I thought she was joking, but her mum and dad were nodding their heads loudly. I looked out of the window. Then it hit me…

They were waiting to see me. This must be how rock stars feel!

'What shall I do?' Chewing on my bottom lip, I needed some older-person wisdom fast. I've always wanted to be more popular, get more friends, but never in my wildest dreams had I thought about being famous.

'It is simple, I will go and talk to them. You stay here,' said Armstrong, unbuckling his seatbelt and walking over to the babbling crowd. He quietened them down, talking to them for two minutes, answering their questions in his wonderful deep, softly-spoken voice.

It worked! They took a last peek before packing up and leaving the scene. Except for one, a creepy-looking alien who stayed at the bottom of the path, watching us as we went in.

Can you believe it, Mum, I'm famous here already! None of us have any idea how they found out about me so quickly, but it feels amazing to be treated like some kind of celebrity.

Armstrong managed to get them to back off. He agreed that I could give an interview at a later date, providing they gave me some space to settle in. I'm walking with a new bounce in my step, and not just because of the lack of gravity.

I'm going on TV next week. ☺

Later that day, we had a visit from the weirdest alien of all – Mr Snotgrass, aka Snottypants' dad. He shuffled along the path as slow as a slug with muscle strain. I spotted him and raced down the stairs to warn the others he was coming. I needn't have bothered. It took him three minutes and twenty-four seconds to get to the front door.

'Who is he?' I asked.

'He is the maximum official person you will encounter here from the Social Care Keepers,' Stella replied. 'He will co-ordinate a conclusion to determine your imminent future.'

'Welcome to Kratos, Esme,' said Mr Snotgrass, as he finally arrived. His hair hung in loose, straggly grey strands. His face was so plump it could be used to advertise pillows.

'I've read your file and decided that you are most welcome to stay with this family. Consider this your home, at least for the time being,' he continued, glancing at Armstrong, who looked down at the floor or his shoes. Or something.

Stella squealed with delight behind me, so I *had* to join in. Rude not to, really!

'You may also attend school with Stella. However, with your permission, we should like to study you. We've never been granted such an opportunity before,' he continued, trying to make himself heard above our girly squeals.

'Whilst my daughter, who I believe you've met, has informed us of humans, we've not experienced one living amongst us. You will provide us with a unique opportunity to better understand your ways. We base much of the structure of our society upon human ideas.'

Well of course I said yes. What's not to like about people being interested in you?

'Well that's splendid, just splendid,' he said beaming at us all. 'To make your stay more comfortable the government has issued a decree which states that all Kratons – should they encounter you – must speak English in your presence. Enjoy your time here, my dear. I will now leave you to acclimatize to your new surroundings.'

We went out that evening for a celebration meal at Lord of the Wings, a chicken restaurant. Armstrong is good friends with the owner, so managed to get us seated at the best table.

People were so rude though, coming right up to our table to stare and poke at me, trying to take selfies. I'm not the one with four eyes, six arms and green skin, so I don't really understand why they bothered. If they wanted something interesting to look at then all they needed to do was pick up a mirror.

*

I love my new home, especially my bedroom. It's at the top of the eastwards spire. It's not got a wardrobe or chest of drawers, but there are secret shelves built into the walls. One push of a button and *hey presto,* they appear.

The bed's a bit weird – a tubey, capsule kind of

thing, hanging on the wall. I've got to pull it down and put it back up again every day. Apparently it's to keep the space dust out, and to be fair there is a lot of it around. It's also got an oxygen supply pumping into it, so I can sleep without a suit on.

AND Stella surprised me by giving me some posters to put up. I've got one of Windzi, Lady Googoo and 4 Minutes of Winter. I was going to put up a Biggy Rage poster, but I went off him last year when he kept losing his tiny temper at the press.

Stella's room is opposite in the westwards spire. We've already been hanging out of the window at night, chucking things across at each other. I'm a better shot than she is, but she is seriously fast. At everything, to be honest.

My room doesn't have time to get messy, thanks to Stella. She blasts in and it's clean in five seconds, so quickly I barely see her move. Think how much money she'd make if she set up a cleaning business in Bournecombe. She'd be a millionaire by Christmas and the whole town would be *sparkling*.

Stella's told me all about a sport they have here, called Swipsling. It's something everybody plays, like skiing in the French Alps, quidditch at Hogwarts etc. I'm going to be getting my own Swipsling kit.

I don't want you to worry about me, Mum. I'm doing fine. I'm not crying myself to sleep any more – I'm not sure you even realised this was happening before I left. Now you know I hope it helps you understand how much happier I am being here.

Gotta scoot, crazy newt. ☺
Esme
x

☆

7

18 January

☆ OOH LOOK, THERE'S
THE ALIEN ☆

☆

Me again. ☺

So anyway, having decided I was staying, it was felt that some celebratory shopping was in order. We travelled two miles across to Area 52 in a Temple of Vroom maxi-taxi. The shopping centre, like everything else here, is huge – a vast titanium building filled with heavenly shops.

We stopped at Noise R Us to pick out some earphones. Then headed to Sparks and Marks for my uniform, followed by H. W. Cliffs for my school supplies. It's weird how quickly I felt at home …

They've bought me my very own kTab, a tiny little tablet which grows bigger when you switch it on. It's essential for life on Kratos. The kids here carry them around, using them in lessons for research, writing up projects, sending in homework etc.

I'm using it to upload these blog posts now, which Stella's shown me how to encrypt so they can only be picked up on Earth. And it's fitted with a tracking device, so that Armstrong and Luna can find me if I ever get lost or in trouble.

Or stolen.

They've let me set up my very own Spacebook account! I've already got tons of friends on there, way more than Stella.

Luna took us to lunch at The Plaice Station where I tried their version of fish and chips. Not nearly as tasty as our chippy, but they still did a fair job.

Oh, and we found the most amazing baker, whose cakes were nearly as good as Gran's. It's called The Bread Pitt. The name seemed familiar, but they assured me it was the only one in the entire universe.

Next stop was the chemist for Luna. She's actually growing the hair on her chin! I mean properly growing it. She gets this gooey paste stuff called *Gone Today, Hair Tomorrow* which she puts on three times a day.

Once she's applied it she has to lie on the sofa for half an hour, waiting for 'the magic' to work. I keep coming across her stretched out. Makes me jump every single time. Chin hair is the height of fashion here – the more the better.

I think we should start a campaign to get Hairy Harrison moved to Kratos. I'm pretty sure she'd be happier, she'd certainly fit in better. They'd have her on the cover of a beauty magazine in the twitch of a whisker.

I'm going to get pocket money every week, providing I help around the house. *Who knew you had to do housework in outer space?* They don't actually have money of course, that's considered too time-consuming to produce and it gets lost or stolen too easily.

They've got what's called the Perihelion Original Orbit Payment System, aka POOPS. I've been given a card which gets loaded with Orbits. Providing I've done my chores, Orbits are transferred from Luna's account every Saturday.

On the way home we visited Back to the Fuschia – a stupendously colourful rock garden centre. We bought some bits and pieces – mostly more rocks – for the back garden. The array of colours was spectacular. It would've made the barrier reef dull in comparison.

Everywhere we went people were calling out and pointing at me, shouting stuff like 'OOH LOOK, THERE'S THE ALIEN!!' and 'LET'S SEE IF WE CAN TOUCH IT!' They buzzed around me like a bunch of bees who've just returned from mining a bumper crop of pollen.

Embarrassing.

It's weird being considered an alien by the very people we consider to be… well, aliens. It's also sad, when you're on your own in a new place, how quickly you can be made to feel like an outsider. I've been lucky, I have Stella and her family, but it must be horrible to be in the same position and not have anyone.

Our last stop was Aerolite to buy my Swipsling. To say I was excited would be an understatement. It was such a tough choice – purple or pink? I went with the pink in the end. Purple *is* my favourite colour, but you *can* have too much of a good thing.

After the shopping trip I was able to have my first go on the Swipsling. The nearest place was the Solstice Organisation for Learning and Rehearsing Swipsling, or SOLARS as everyone calls it.

I went into the beginner's class of course, with Stella coming to give me support. It was held in an enormous crater on the outskirts of the city. We heard it before we saw it. There were so many squeals and shrieks coming from behind the 6.8-metre entrance gates. Walking in, I gasped.

Stella grinned at me. 'It is exceptionally spectacular, is it not?'

The crater's diameter was at least 350 metres, bigger than the biggest football stadium, with twice as many spotlights. It was divided into different sections. Towering above each section was a series of gargantuan metal arms, from which dangled steel ropes with shiny hooks on the end. The whole scene looked like a thousand sparkly Christmas tree decorations suspended over a rocky football pitch.

Across from the entrance stood a group of girls, chattering away. As soon as they saw us they stopped talking and turned their backs. Stella pretended not to notice, but a blue flush on her face told me she had.

'Who are they?'

'Merely a variety of girls from my…
our educational establishment. You will encounter them tomorrow, no doubt.'

'How do these things work?' I asked, trying to distract her. I really couldn't wait to have a go.

'Those support rods,' she said, pointing at the metal arms, 'grasp the bouncer ropes, with which it is necessary to connect our Swipslings. Come, let us proceed to the attachment station and commence our experience.'

It looked scary the way they were bouncing around – knocking into each other – so I stood and watched Stella for the first part of the lesson. She is soooooo good at it, eclipsing everyone with her supersonic skills.

She can twirl, circle and loop the loop, turning upside down in the flick of an eye. She makes Delicious Dylan's skateboarding skills look amateur by comparison.

I would've carried on watching her for the second part of the lesson, but the instructor made her sit down because she was 'distracting everybody'. Personally, I think the instructor was jealous – she was clearly much better than him.

Pretty soon it was my go, so I buckled up and did what the instructor told me to do – 'hold on to the side and *be the rope*'. I bobbed about for most of the time, hanging on for dear life.

It was hard to emotionally connect with the rope when I felt like one of Gran's teabags on a string, dunked up and down, again and again, until all the flavour was squished out. I couldn't bring myself to let go of the side – I was way too scared I'd ping off into outer space.

This had looked easy when I arrived, but think I'm going to need a few more lessons before I'm let loose into the middle of the crater. Just yo-yoing close to the perimeter left me feeling as if my internal organs had been playing a game of 'tag' and had swapped locations in my body.

Or something like that.

It didn't help that I'd sensed someone was watching me, but whenever I turned around, there was no one there. Everyone seemed caught up in their own activity.

'It is perfectly acceptable, Esme. You will undoubtedly become immune to the deep trepidation you are experiencing in time.' She was trying to make me feel better, but failing miserably. I don't like to be beaten by anything so I can't wait to come back and try it again.

As we walked towards the entrance, I glanced back and spotted someone following us. Whispering to Stella, I grabbed her, pulling her behind one of the booths that was selling food.

We popped our heads out to check what he was doing. He'd stopped in his tracks, peering around, a confused look on his face. Thirty-one seconds later he walked off.

'That's the same guy who was hanging around the house when I arrived. Who is he?'

'I am not convinced I am familiar with his facial features,' she said. 'However, it is apparent he may be connected to a new exhibition being built, situated to the west of the city. His uniform is recognisable as such. Father is permitted to acquire tickets, therefore we will undoubtedly visit it once it is completed.'

'Why would he be following *us*?'

'Perhaps he is captivated by the notion of observing a real human being? He will be harmless, of this I am assured. It matters not, for returning to our abode is imperative.' She pushed one of her right arms through mine.

'Father and Mother will compel us to retire to our bedrooms without delay tonight. An early rise tomorrow morning is essential if we wish to make great achievements in our educational progress.'

Having double-checked he'd gone, we slipped out of our hiding place and made our way to the Jetcar park, where we climbed into a maxi-taxi and headed home.

Looking posh, orange squash. ☺

Esme

x

8

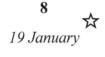

19 January

Vigilance is required

So anyway, I started at Ashtron Community School today. It was so exciting!

I cannot believe I just used the words 'school' and 'exciting' in the same sentence together.

The school is in an area on the outskirts of the city. Walking through the doors I was overwhelmed with how small I was.

I *was* nervous, worrying the students wouldn't like me. How wrong can you be?

They loved me!! I'm such a novelty to them. They've never had a student from Earth before, so they were as enthusiastic me.

Once inside I was hit by the same noise and bustle I'm used to at Markham High. The Populars were already congregating at the end of the hall, huddled around each other, creating a tight circle. Occasionally they deigned to look at the rest of us. One of them spotted me and rattled off something to her crew, who all, in unison, looked at me.

And.

Smiled.

Since when did The Populars smile at me? This whole experience keeps getting stranger by the minute.

As they made their way over to me, Stella whispered, 'Complete vigilance is required. This collection of girls in my species can be highly untrustworthy.'

'Yep, we've got them on Earth too, remember?'

'Affirmative, I have perceived this. The one located in the central section provides them with commands. Aurora 17,678,' she said. 'Her discourteous behaviour has brought distress to me on many occasions. Maximum humiliation occurs when she neglects to extend an invitation to me for one of her social gatherings.'

Awkward.

At this point I was saved from certain friendship death by the headteacher. 'Welcome, Esme 1, I've been so looking forward to meeting you. My name is Mrs Wobbleton,' she said, a great white smile circling her face.

'And, Stella, may I take this opportunity to congratulate you on your successful mission to Planet Earth,' she continued, one eye on us, the other three twirling everywhere else.

Looking at Stella's face, which had gone a deep shade of blue, I wondered what I'd missed. She rushed off and left me standing with Mrs Wobbleton.

Bum.

My worries about the headteacher disappeared

fairly quickly when she gave me a tour of the school. *See, this is how it should be done, not making a student do it.*

She actually seemed OK, in an 'I'm an alien headteacher' kind of way. But I still wasn't comfortable with the fact that she has four eyes. Waaaay too much spying equipment for one teacher.

And she has this gargantuan mouth, which I can't take my eyes off. When she speaks her lips kind of undulate, like a jellyfish's bottom. Fascinating, yet fearsome, all at the same time.

As she deposited me back with Stella six minutes and thirty-four seconds later she shook my hand, nearly squeezing the life out of it.

Watching her walk away, her blue hair flicking back and forth, I spotted a small tattoo behind her ear – a circle with an eye at its centre. The folds of her neck were moving, making it look like the eye was winking at me. *Blimey, this is one teacher who really does have eyes at the back of her head!*

I stopped thinking about it when I found out that the first lesson of the day was history. My favourite!

*

The teacher looked as if he'd probably witnessed most of the events he taught.

'Well, now for your presentations,' said Mr Crustyman, after the fuss of my arrival had died down. 'I'd like you to share the research you completed for homework last week. Keep it short, as I want everyone to have an opportunity to speak.'

The first three students spoke on a number of topics. Stella looked bored silly, which I thought was unreasonable, as they were really entertaining. Especially Star 557,079, whose talk was about Neil Armstrong's moon landing in 1969. We think of him as a hero, but every time Star put up a photo, the class sniggered. They think the spaceship Armstrong travelled on was really outdated.

By the time they got to the picture of Armstrong standing on the moon, the whole class – bar me and Stella – were pretty much rolling on the floor with laughter. This upset Star so much she couldn't finish her presentation. I felt properly bad for her, but in the end even I couldn't stop myself grinning. Laughter is so infectious.

Anyway, when the fourth student got up to present I noticed a distinct change in Stella. She sat bolt upright, ruffled her pink hair and suddenly became focused.

'Thank you, Obi, please proceed,' encouraged the teacher.

'I researched how Kratons came to live here,' he began. 'Everybody knows we arrived 542 years ago from Planet Hyperion, which is part of the Saturnian system. What is little understood is the real reason. Many claim the planet was destroyed, leaving us with no choice but to flee, building a new life here on Kratos. However, there are theories arising which shed new light onto the reasons for the migration.'

He paused, looking at Mr Crustyman, before continuing. 'Some believe the relocation was a direct result of a disagreement between the two brothers who ruled Hyperion at the time – Saros 1 and Martius 1. The dispute escalated to the degree that our noble ancestor, Saros 1, left Hyperion to establish a new colony on Kratos.

'When he left, he took with him the famous "24", who formed the basis of the Kraton society we recognise today. They'd hoped one day to be reunited with the people they left behind, but sadly this was not to be. It is believed that Hyperion simply vanished after a gigantic asteroid smashed into it. Of course we can't be sure nobody survived, but experts agree that it seems unlikely.'

'Interesting, interesting,' said Mr Crustyman, removing a crumb from his beard, looking the exact opposite of interested. 'I would be fascinated to know where you got your information from, Obi.' Without waiting for a response, he invited the next student to give her talk.

Stella watched Obi return to his seat. When she realised I was watching her, she looked down and pretended to shuffle some books around on her desk.

I understood then – Obi is Stella's 'Delicious Dylan'. I may not possess the greatest skills in the romance department, but I've decided to bring these two together.

We sat in the corner of the dining hall at lunch – a gigantic cave with huge lights hanging from the ceiling, like 104 droopy bats stretching out, after a long night's sleep. There were six people eating at the table, but we were on our own within three minutes, eighteen seconds.

I was expecting to be hassled all day, but here's the funny thing – nobody really bothered us. Stella doesn't appear to have any friends at all. It's not just The Populars who don't like her, everyone gives her a wide berth. I couldn't understand why, so I asked Obi at second break what the problem was.

'Simple,' he said. 'It's because she's so clever. The others get fed up with the teachers making a fuss of her. And nobody likes a know-it-all.'

'That's unfair, it's not like she can help being clever,' I said.

'I agree, and it wouldn't be such a big deal, but she's not even in the right year group. She jumped a year. She's younger than all of us.'

'But she's so lovely.'

'You're sure about that, are you?' He sauntered off. Rhetorical questions can be handy, but when someone uses them to dodge stuff, they're rubbish. I've got no choice but to trust her, but, if I'm being honest, I do feel uneasy.

Anyway, got to dash as I'm cooking supper for Stella's family and friends tonight. I'm making a spaghetti bolognese, using the secret recipe Gran taught me.

Give my love to Maisie and Isaac. Tell Isaac to behave himself. Hope he's enjoying playschool and not bossing the other kids around too much. Oh, and tell Maisie she can keep my pink glittery nail varnish I left behind, that's if she's not already taken ownership of it!

All OK, lemon soufflé. ☺
Esme
   x

9

19 January

Shooting stars, Celeste

Ha ha ha ha ha ha ha ha ha ha ha.

Supper was hysterical! I've never seen so much mess in all my life. They've never had spaghetti bolognese before. I *cannot* wait to cook it again. It wasn't helped by the fact that their pasta is 75.4cm long. Imagine that being swirled around on a plate by five green aliens, before they attempt to fit it in their gargantuan mouths. And missing, naturally. These guys make Isaac look like he's spent a year at a Swiss finishing school.

I was shocked by the friends who came for supper, and not just because they were big and green. I'm used to that now. Rather, it was *who* the friends were – Mrs Wobbleton, in a killer whale of a black and white dress, and her husband.

Mr Wobbleton is different to Mrs 'call me Celeste' Wobbleton. When he talks it doesn't look like he's about to gobble you up. *And* he doesn't have a strange tattoo on the back of his neck. I know because I accidentally on purpose climbed on my chair to adjust a mirror on the wall to sneak a peek.

They asked me loads of weird questions. I was OK with the 'Are you happy?' and 'What is your favourite part about life on Kratos?' questions. It was when they started asking me stuff about you, Maisie and Isaac that I started to get stressed.

They wondered if you'd ever come and live here. I said you'd probably prefer to stay on Earth for now as you're quite fond of breathing without a spacesuit on. Don't worry, they're not about to come back and snatch you. At least I don't think they are.

In between slurping their food and cleaning themselves up, the conversation became a whole lot more interesting...

'We're very pleased, it's the first time there's been a school trip to the Floating Hills in thirty years,' said Mrs Wobbleton, her four eyes rolling round and round like a washing machine on a spin cycle, making themselves, and me, dizzy.

'I trust the correct precautions will be in place, as discussed,' said Armstrong. Up until this point the evening had been light-hearted, but the mood suddenly changed.

'Well of course, we've conducted all the necessary risk assessments, we won't tolerate a repeat of thirty years ago,' she replied.

'Good, good, pleased to hear it,' he said, sounding anything *but* pleased.

'What exactly happened thirty years ago?'

They turned to look at me, apart from Luna, who

arched her eyebrows at her husband. 'Well— '

'What happened, Esme, was an unmitigated disaster, said Mrs Wobbleton. 'However, it was completely out of the school's control, so I fail to see why Armstrong is making such a fuss.'

'If my girls are going on a school trip to the Floating Hills, I have every right to "make a fuss",' he said, tapping the table with a fork. '*Shooting stars,* Celeste, you know exactly why I'm concerned. Stop brushing the issue under the carpet!'

'Now, now, Armstrong dear,' said Luna. 'I'm sure the staff have done everything in their power to ensure the students' safety.'

'Yes, you're absolutely right Luna,' Mrs Wobbleton butted in again. 'We've spent weeks putting this trip together. Your children will be perfectly safe, have no fear.'

Why was Armstrong getting his big alien-sized knickers in a twist over a simple school trip?

'Yes, but what actually happened? Can somebody please tell me?' I asked again.

Another thing I've learned since I've been here is that wherever in the universe you travel, you will always find adults who ignore kids.

'Um… er… would anyone care for some more juice?' asked Mr Wobbleton diplomatically.

'Why thank you, that would be marvellous,' said Luna, before whispering, 'Stella, maybe you'd better explain things to Esme. If you like, you can go and get ready for bed now.'

After we'd excused ourselves we ran upstairs.

'You must increase your acceleration! Come and inhabit my bedroom for a brief interval before retiring,' she called from her room.

'I'm coming, I'm coming,' I shouted, before slumping onto her bed. 'Now *please* tell me what happened. And *please* explain why your dad starts flapping like a chicken trying to win a chicken flapping competition whenever someone mentions the Floating Hills. I know there was that business with his dad years ago, but his reaction is a bit over the top.'

'You must comprehend there is an exceedingly worthy explanation for his elevated anxiety,' she said. 'His experiences from thirty years past have left a dread of the Floating Hills.'

'So thirty years ago something bad happened?'

'Affirmative. Ashtron Community School developed prominence in the national news. Unfortunately, the news was highly negative,' she said, her voice dropping to nearly a whisper. 'The annual school excursion to the Floating Hills was attended by my father and his brother, Kepler 45,092.

'My father reports that the day had commenced in a competent fashion. There was much exhilaration amongst the students. Indeed our students are not dissimilar to students on Earth. They propelled foodstuffs and beverages diagonally across the Space Bus,' she paused, smiling. 'However, events were soon to alter their buoyant spirits.'

She stopped, staring at the floor for four seconds.

'You don't have to tell me if it's upsetting you too

much. I can ask your dad to tell me.'

She looked up sharply. 'Negative! Circumstances should never permit you to harass him into full disclosure of particular details of this incident. It would greatly distress him.'

'What happened? It must have been really awful.'

'The students were instructed to remain on the lower level of the first hill. However, two students disobeyed, and ascended the hill in search of adventure. One of them was never seen again.'

'Oh no! What happened to the other one?'

'The other student returned. His name is Armstrong. My father. The student who disappeared was his younger brother, Kepler.' She waited a moment to allow the information to sink in.

'There have been a significant number of rumours regarding his whereabouts. The most prominent theory is that he was abducted by a faction of the Bad Ones.'

'Why would they pick on a little boy? That's just so wrong.'

'Affirmative, he was merely a child. However, as you know, my grandfather was a famous Justice Keeper at this point in our history. It has been suggested that the Bad Ones captured Kepler in vengeful retribution, quite likely someone he dispatched to the Outlands.'

'Surely they went to look for him?' I asked.

'Countless search parties were launched over the ensuing months. However, negative trace of him was discovered. My grandfather relinquished his employment. He would never function as a Justice Keeper again.

'My father has never stopped censuring himself. He considers himself entirely responsible. When his reaction is contextualised, it becomes understandable to comprehend his torment.'

I promised her I wouldn't mention it to Armstrong again. It just goes to show what Gran used to say is true, 'nobody knows what's going on in other people's lives, everyone's got their struggles'.

*

As I settled down into my own bed later, I couldn't help feeling sorry for Armstrong. It can't have been easy losing a sibling. I know I chose to 'lose' mine, but it doesn't stop me missing them.

I hope we're still allowed to go on the school trip. He's meeting with Mrs Wobbleton to 'further discuss the security arrangements', so I'm keeping my fingers and everything else crossed it'll be fine. I hope he can find a way to let go of the past and not let it spoil the present.

I love the way Armstrong and Luna are together. He's so helpful, always checking she is OK, doing little things to make her smile. It made me sad today, thinking of you not having that kind of person in your life.

The longest boyfriend you had after Maisie and Isaac's dad, was for seven months. Dave the Rave. He treated you well to start with. But then you found him in your best friend's house with no good reason, *and* he tried to apologise by bringing you a super-sized packet of crisps. Nothing says sorry quite like a packet of crisps, right Mum?

I think if you'd met someone who'd taken care of you properly, you might have been happier. And we might have got on better…

Keeping well, mademoiselle. ☺

Love,

Esme

xx

10

21 January

Never say never

Can't believe Stella might be Head Girl!

Today in assembly they announced nominations were open for 'the prestigious roles of Head Girl and Head Boy'.

'Naturally, the staff have already submitted their own nomination,' Mrs Wobbleton announced from the stage, the smile basking on her face strangely hypnotic. 'Stella 12,614, you've been nominated by us due to your outstanding academic performance, over and above your years, and your unswerving commitment to the school's vision of inclusivity for all. Regardless of creed, race or species.'

A collective groan rang out from the entire school – including me. As big a compliment as this was, it clearly wasn't going to help Stella one little bit in the popularity stakes. The students in this school have no appreciation of how wonderful she is.

Something needs to be done, and I'm just the person for the job. I'm going to be her campaign manager. What do aliens want in a Head Girl? To find out the answer I set about undertaking some alien market research, putting together a questionnaire:

1.What skills you would most value in a Head Girl?

2.What values do you feel are the most important?

3.If you were going to choose a candidate to vote for, what might persuade you to do so?

4.What would you like to see changed in school?

I collected a few and wasn't surprised to see the usual stuff there. New toilets. New lockers. New dining hall. All of them wanted the teachers to stop picking Stella for the best projects and awards. One boy said he would vote for her if she could get Mrs Wobbleton to agree to ban homework.

Dream on.

One girl said she actually quite liked her, adding, 'I wonderful, Stella is best Head Girl, for the candidate think.' I wondered who wrote that…

Another girl said she'd vote for her if she agreed to leave the school! This isn't going to be an easy job.

The first step is to make her cooler. Now I know you'd probably argue that there's not a lot you can do with a 2.24-metre alien, but I firmly believe in the old saying 'never say never'.

At lunch I decided to tackle the tricky subject. Despite her calm composure, she gets really touchy when I try to talk to her about 'situation no friends'.

'Stella,' I said, drawing a chair up a little closer to her in the cavernous dining hall. 'What's the most important thing about school for you?'

'Naturally, the extension of my learning.' She looked at me as if I'd just asked her the stupidest question in the universe.

'If you could change anything, what would it be?' I was trying to sound casual.

'I have great perception regarding the direction of this conversation.' A stern look crossed her face. 'This topic has been deliberated previously, and I consider the issue of my peer group acceptance closed for eternity.'

'I'm sorry, it's just that I know it upsets you. You keep it in too much. Please let me help?' She took my hand in one of hers and squeezed it tightly.

Taking it as a sign of encouragement, I raced on, 'So, I thought your mum and dad could maybe let us have a party at your house. They can go out, or stay upstairs, and we—'

'Negative, noisy social gatherings are not permitted,' she said, horror written all over her face and squirming through her body. 'A previous event terminated in disaster. The house was unoccupied, individuals failed to make an appearance. To this day the sound of silence remains lodged within my brain cells. A great necessity for counselling followed this event.'

'OK, scrap the party idea. How about you become a cheerleader? I've seen the team here, they're really good. You could properly show them how it's done.'

'I have deep concerns that you are perhaps misjudging my physical prowess, Esme,' she said, laughing. 'Why, if you requested me to enrol in the History Club, I would comprehend, and fathom your logic.'

'But you're the fastest person I know!'

'Mere rapidity is no recompense for lack of co-ordination.'

'How's about you start using your special gift? I bet that'd make them sit up and take notice.'

'Sadly, you are correct. However, as I explained in Bournecombe, it is merely the teachers who appreciate my gift. My peers... well, they appear to be resentful of the attention I receive because of it. It is appropriate that I suppress it, unless circumstances dictate it necessary to use.'

'Well how about we do something with your appearance? I could pierce your ears?!'

She looked at me, and suddenly smiled. 'I have discerned that your popular peers on Earth have these shiny items suspended from their ears.'

'Yes, you can even have mine. They're yours, just say the word!'

'I have contemplated and deduced that these *earrings* would ensure an immense improvement to my image and potentially generate great respect from my peers. Are you in agreement?'

'Yessss!' I shrieked, getting way too much attention from other students. 'Of course, you'll be the first person to ever have them on Kratos. A trendsetter. What a great idea! Come on, let's go now.'

We headed straight to the embroidery classroom. They're nuts about tapestry here, it's compulsory for everyone to learn. Even the boys.

Random.

Anyway, I got onto the chair to reach her left ear,

but she was quivering so much she nearly shook me off. 'Hold still, Stella, I can't do it if you're going to make such a fuss.'

'You can assure me I will not experience intense agony, Esme?' she asked, not sounding in the least bit enthusiastic about the plan to make her look cooler than all of the cool girls put together. Or the fact that I was sacrificing the gold star earrings Gran gave me.

'I must refrain from bleeding, for to do so will result in maximum quantities of blood,' she said, quivering. 'Upon consideration, I wish to retract my agreement to your proposal.'

'Don't panic, it'll be fine. When I had mine done there was no blood at all.'

Finally, having managed to get her to stay still, I pushed the needle into her earlobe.

The scream was so loud, I'm sure it could be heard far away and over the Floating Hills.

Then the blood came. Buckets of it.

That's when she fainted, pulling me down with her. Fortunately, having heard the noise, half the school had gathered outside to investigate. Obi barged into the room.

He managed to calm Stella down, sending a younger student for the school nurse. In the blink of four eyes, she was whisked away to the school office, where she was bandaged up.

My first attempt to improve her popularity hasn't gone down so well, at school or at home. I thought I was doing her a favour, but it's safe to say her mum and dad definitely didn't appreciate it.

How was I supposed to know if their skin is punctured they won't stop bleeding for hours? It's not like I'm some kind of expert alientologist. And who knew aliens grounded kids?! I'm not allowed out now for two days, not even for my Swipsling lesson! I'm starting to feel like I'm at home again.

But it wasn't a complete waste of time – Stella and Obi seem much closer.

Result.

*

I've been working my way through my chocolate stash, but I'm worried it's going to run out soon. I can't get my hands on any decent chocolate here, all they've got is one crumby brand – *Mercury Bar* – which looks like chocolate, but tastes like a monkey's butt. Not that I've ever actually tasted a monkey's butt, I need to add!

Yuck.

They've said I *can* go out to do the TV interview for *The Rodney Swineheart Show* tomorrow. The one Armstrong promised the reporters when I first arrived. I *CANNOT* wait, it's going to be amazing to be on TV.

I'm going to be famous!

Better sprint, peppermint. ☺

Love,

Esme

xx

11

☆

22 January

☆*Global freezing is a very real threat*

☆

☆

I do *NOT* want to be famous!

I went to the TV studios with Stella, Armstrong and Luna. Obi was the 'extra guest', chosen for obvious reasons. *wiggles eyebrows suggestively*

'Obi, you sit next to Stella,' I said, climbing into the back of the Jetcar. 'I need to sit near the window to look out for any alien activity,' I said, giggling at my own joke. Watching the passing scenery, I pretended to ignore everyone, but secretly listened to the conversations.

I've got no skills when it comes to boys, as you've no doubt guessed, Mum, but what limited tips I've picked up from you, I passed on to her. That is, after I finally got her to admit she had a crush on him. He couldn't resist my invitation and they seemed to get on like a house on fire.

After what felt like forever we finally arrived. I don't think I've ever been so excited before... well, apart from the time that Gran took me to see *Jason and His Amazing Technicolour Phantom Cats of the Opera* at the theatre. It was wicked.

It was made even more fun because Gran joined in by chucking bits of popcorn over the heads of the people in front. Then she stuck some up her nose and pretended to be a creature from outer space, wobbling her head from side to side, cross-eyed and tongue lolling out from one side of her mouth. I'll never forget the look on the faces of the two people in front of us.

Hilarious. ☺

Outside the studio we were treated to the most incredible sight – hundreds of aliens waiting to see me. As the Jetcar pulled up they made a big rush towards us. Fortunately they were blocked by security guards, the biggest aliens I've ever seen in my life. They had muscles as big as a hippo's bum.

They bundled us through the door as quickly as they could. Only one person got close enough to grab my sleeve, but I shook her off. They were calling my name like I was some kind of superstar.

One even held out her baby, shouting, 'Esme, Esme, please touch my baby. I've named her after you!'

It would've been flattering, but it's not such a great honour when you consider my name was being given to a child who was a rather unattractive shade of bogie green.

Rodney's assistant was waiting for us in the corridor leading to the main recording area. Obi, Stella and her family went through to sit in the studio, but I had to stay to chat through stuff.

Within four seconds of them going through Stella came back, squealing with excitement. 'Esme, what is your speculation about the composition of the audience?!'

'I don't have any idea who is in the audience,' I replied. I've only lived here a few days, I don't quite know what she was expecting from me.

'Only Eclipse Total!' she said, with the starstruckiest look on her face. 'She is a singer who has astonishing vocal range and talent. She causes all other singers on Kratos to remain in the shade!' Her excitement was infectious, so I quickly sneaked a peek.

The front row was full of VIPs, and in the middle of them was the most sparkling alien in the entire universe. She was beautiful – a wonderful, glittery, bearded soufflé.

I'd seen her picture in the magazine which Stella sometimes bought, and heard some of her music, which leaves a lot to be desired. She does a lot of work for charity though, supporting Jabba the Cutt, which provides haircuts for aliens who can't afford them. Their hair grows at 4.3 times the rate of ours, so they need more regular visits to the hairdresser.

The audience got to their feet as Rodney's assistant and me made our way into the studio, at which point Eclipse walked over to us.

'Hello Esme, my name is Eclipse, I've been so looking forward to meeting you. I'm interested in the planet that you come from. I cannot wait to hear about your life,' she said breathily, as she reached out one of her right hands to shake mine.

'Tha— thank you, it's um… not easy coming from Planet Earth,' I stuttered, not quite sure what to say or do. Stella tugged at my sleeve. 'Um… have you met Stella yet?'

'No, I don't believe I have,' she said. 'Say, aren't you that girl who brought the human to Kratos?'

Stella, whose eyes were doing double somersaults, could barely get a response out. 'Um… cr… affirmative. It was… um... providential that I was selected for the STAR Programme. I highly regard your singing, Eclipse. Your compositions contain great eloquence and harmony.'

'Why thank you. You've done Kratos an amazing service. I'm a patron of the STAR Programme. It's doing an amazing job finding answers to the problems our planet is facing today,' said Eclipse. 'Global freezing is a very real threat, and humans on Earth have proven brilliant at warming their planet up. We can learn a lot from them.'

Stella grinned the whole time Eclipse was speaking, nodding her head, lapping up every word that fell from her mouth.

'I trust you have been provided with an opportunity to demonstrate your exceedingly inordinate capacity for musical performance tonight?' Stella asked.

'No, I'm sorry, but I'm just here to listen to Esme tonight,' she said. Noticing her disappointment, she quickly added, 'But don't worry, I'm performing at the concert hall next month, so why don't you come along? I'll have my agent send you some VIP tickets.'

With that she sashayed back to her seat. Right next to Mrs Wobbleton, who was in a frilly dress, a row of sharp sequins along the hem. Within two seconds they were deep in conversation. Who'd have thought *they'd* have anything in common. And Stella could at least have warned me I was entering into Wobbleton-infested waters!

Rodney Swineheart was on stage, having his make-up and hair done by two girls. He looked very glam in his red glittery suit, designer glasses and white, waist-length ponytail. He soon swatted the girls away, pulling out a mirror to admire himself, running his tongue over his sparkling teeth, pulling bits of food out from between them.

Gross.

One of the studio directors called me to my seat. Nibbling at one of my nails, I hesitated for three seconds before stepping onto the stage, wondering what the next hour would bring…

*

'Ladies and Gentlemen, welcome to a very special edition of *The Rodney Swineheart Show*,' said Rodney, as the cameras and autocue started to roll.

'Today is a very special occasion with a very special guest. Yes, today I'm thrilled to welcome the very first human alien to our show. All the way from Planet Earth, Ladies and Gentlemen, please give a warm welcome to Esme 1!'

Everyone stood to clap. I should've been happy,

I know, but all I could think was – *Actually no, my name is Esme Amelia Tickle!* I didn't say anything though. I just carried on smiling and waving at them, with a sinking feeling in my stomach.

'Esme, we want to hear about what it's like living on Planet Earth. Through our STAR Programme we've learned such a lot, but we recognize we still have much to learn…'

Blah, blah, blah.

On and on he went, not giving me a chance to say anything, until *finally* – 'So tell us, what *is* the best thing about living on Planet Earth?'

'Well, I think the best thing has got to be the food. You see, in England we've got all kinds of crisps and chocolate, and I kind of miss them. And of course my mum, she's wonderful,' I replied, wondering where that had come from. 'We've also got the best beaches! Bournecombe has an amazing one. People surf and snorkel all day in the ocean.'

'Yes I've seen pictures of these *beaches*. Tell me, why would you want to take most of your clothes off to stand in water all day, leaving your skin crinkled and finding sand in unmentionable places?' Rodney asked, swivelling to give a megawatt smile and wink at the audience, prompting them to laugh hysterically.

'You wouldn't understand unless you'd tried, it's the best fun ever. I love swimming.' I was starting to feel like I truly *was* an alien in this world.

'This has puzzled us on Kratos. It certainly doesn't look like fun,' he continued with his saccharine smile, which was really starting to get on my nerves.

'People get knocked over by waves in these oceans, stung by jellyfish, attacked by killer sharks. You humans are indeed curious creatures.'

This, coming from a 2.56-metre six-armed, four-eyed alien.

The irony.

'Well what about the animals on Earth, they're amazing.' He was making so many digs about Earth, I wanted to defend it. 'I don't see many interesting creatures around these parts.'

Looking around the audience, I wondered if this was actually such a good argument.

'Yes, yes, we are indeed fascinated by your animals. This is why the STAR Programme has funded the construction of the Planet Earth Exhibition,' he said. At this the audience got to their feet, clapping, whooping and cheering furiously.

'What's this Planet Earth Exhibition?' I asked, once the noise had died down.

'It's a special project we are building, which will house examples of animals from your planet. It will be open to the general public soon,' he replied.

I was a bit gobsmacked, because although I'd heard about the new exhibition, nobody had mentioned that it was about Planet Earth. I tried to get more information from him, but he kept moving the conversation back to 'Esme's Story'. I couldn't believe no one had told me.

By the time I finished the interview, I was beginning to feel uncomfortable with the attention I was getting. Something didn't feel right – it still doesn't – but I can't put my finger on it.

I've been invited to appear on some other shows. They've asked me to be a judge on *Surely Kratos Must Have Some Talent Somewhere*. And they're trying to get me to be a special guest on the *Strictly Great Kratos Celebrity Wake Off*, where celebrities compete to see who can stay awake the longest. I've turned them both down though, as I've completely gone off the idea of being famous.

One good thing to come out of today is that Obi and Stella are getting on like a house on fire. I think spending time with her outside of school has helped him see her in a different light. He's not the only one with changing perspectives...

Gotta dash, potato mash. ☹

Love,

Esme

xx

12

26 January

Why, have you visited a rainforest?

Had *the* most amazing day today. It started out really boring. Luna had us doing some work in the garden, which actually just involved moving rocks around. Nothing too hardcore.

After lunch Stella and me had to report to Armstrong about our week at school. Both of us were keen to show off, because we got top marks in our maths exam.

'Show me your books, girls,' said Armstrong, before we whipped them out of our bags and raced to get to him first. Stella won.

Standard.

'Well done, I'm very pleased,' he said, leafing through both of our books slowly. 'I have to say, when you first arrived I had concerns that you might prove to be a distraction for Stella, but it seems you have been quite the opposite.' Which completely made me blush. 'So, I've decided to take you out this afternoon, to somewhere that may become very important to you, Esme. The Planet Earth Exhibition is calling.'

'Yesssss!' We jumped up and down, squealing.

'It's not finished yet, but it's a good idea for Esme to have a look around in adva—'

'Why don't you girls go and get ready,' suggested Luna, frowning at Armstrong.

'That is certainly a magnificent notion,' said Stella, grabbing me by the hand, nearly pulling me over as we ran up the stairs.

The exhibition centre is on the other side of the city, so we had to pack for a long journey. Nine minutes and forty-two seconds later we arrived.

It was obvious it still had a bit of work to be done. Parts of the roof were missing, and there were several panels missing from the front entrance, but it still looked impressive.

Positioned above the entrance was a symbol – a circle with an eye in the middle of it. Just like the one Mrs Wobbleton has on the back of her neck. How on Kratos is she connected to *this* place?

I pushed all other thoughts aside as we walked towards the building. It felt like the windows were glowering at us as we approached.

The man who ushered us in was instantly recognisable. He was the one I'd seen following us during my first Swipsling lesson. He didn't speak, but his badge told us his name was Sputnik 5,655. His uniform told us he didn't like ironing.

I nudged Stella. She looked at me and raised her eyebrows in an 'I told you so' kind of way. I guess she was right about him being harmless, but it didn't alter the fact he'd properly spooked me at the time.

It's much bigger inside than it looks on the outside. The centre opens up at the back to gigantic patches of land, which will have loads of zones showing different things from life on Earth.

Each of them is covered by a massive bubble of Perspex, which keeps the oxygen in. I don't know how many there were, having zoned out before I'd finished counting.

We went to the 'Meet the Rainforest' zone first. We found some tamarin monkeys, who didn't look best happy, sitting in some fake trees. There was an artificial waterfall in the background, splishing and sploshing down into a fake rock pool. The stench was awful.

Buzzing around the plants were some hummingbirds, sounding way more in tune than Eclipse did when she sang.

The sign read:

Welcome to the Rainforest. In this zone you will see a small selection of animals and birds which live in the tropical rainforests of Planet Earth. These forests can be found throughout the planet, and hold 82% of all known creatures.

'Who put this information together?' I asked, turning around to nobody in particular. 'I bet my shiny new Swipsling it's someone who's never been to Earth.'

'I did,' said a deep voice.

Turning around, I spotted someone sloping

towards us. It was the stalker, showing off a set of wonky yellow teeth, which seemed to be attempting an escape bid from his mouth.

'Please allow me to introduce myself,' he said. 'I am Sputnik 5,655, the director of this exhibition. Pleased to make with the acquaintance.'

'This information is ridiculous. Everybody knows only around 51% of the Earth's animals live in the rainforest, not 82%.'

Sputnik studied me with hooded eyes the colour of stagnant pondweed. 'Why, have you visited a rainforest? My understanding is that you come from a location on Earth where no such place exists.'

Smug.

'We do have books, you know. And the internet. Not to mention zoos, which are highly informative.'

'Come, let us depart from this section and transport ourselves over to the English Farmyard Zone,' Stella said, grabbing my arm and moving me towards the door. But not so fast that I didn't notice Sputnik stop and whisper something to Armstrong.

'I wonder what animals they've managed to get into here,' I said, as we made our way towards the life-sized, dung-coloured plastic cow. It had a sign draped round its neck reading – *English Farm Adventures: this way…*

Since when did anyone have an adventure on an English farm, Mum? The only time we ever visited one, Isaac spent the entire time on the ground pulling out worms. This was followed by a screaming fit after I told him that worms couldn't be his best friends as they don't have brains.

Then he escaped from us, ran into a cow field and promptly fell into a pile of fresh cow poo. The sticky kind. Eurgh... think I need to change the subject.

The 'farmyard' zone had some of the usual creatures – turkeys gobbling their food, several lame ducks and chickens busy looking for their eggs, which they'd somehow mislaid.

I had no beef with the cows, but the skinny horse didn't seem in the least bit stable. The pigs looked completely bored. The four sheep, by sheer coincidence, looked very similar. Everything was lovely and perfectly fitting, until, that is, we got to the two parrots.

I mean, have you ever seen parrots on a farm???? They looked so stupid. I dissolved into fits of giggles, which quickly turned into tears. It all just reminded me of home so much.

The only thing that cheered me up was the promise of ice-cream later. When you consider that the word 'stressed' is desserts spelt backwards, is there any wonder ice-cream makes me feel so happy?

We moved around the rest of the exhibition fairly quickly. To be honest there's not an awful lot to see at the moment. They're gradually adding different exhibits as each zone is finished. Apparently they're bringing some alligators from Florida in next week, when the next group returns from its mission.

Maybe they'll be going into the massive enclosure I saw being built at the other end of the building.

Definitely something important going into that one. It's floor-to-ceiling Plexiglas, with visibility on three sides.

As we left I had that weird feeling of being watched again. Sure enough as I turned around there was Sputnik, his four eyes following us to our Jetcar.

'He gives me the creeps,' I said to Stella. 'And why does that symbol keep popping up everywhere?' I asked, pointing to the sign above the entrance.

'It is merely a sign to represent this exhibition.'

'Mrs Wobbleton has it tattooed on the back of her neck. I wonder what her connection is.'

'Come on, girls, we need to hurry. Supper will be ready soon,' interrupted Armstrong, gesturing for us to get into the Jetcar. 'We'll have to come back again when the exhibition is finished.'

I think once they get their facts right, the Planet Earth Exhibition will be an amazing place, Mum. I never understood why you and Protest Pete made such a fuss about zoos. I mean, they teach people so much about the natural world. Surely that can't be wrong? And when you see how excited the children are… well, I just don't get it. Sorry.

I don't actually want to come home, but I'm definitely feeling a homesick. I guess visiting the exhibition today has stirred things up a bit.

Think I need to get a grip.

Good news though. Armstrong has finally agreed to let us go on the school trip to the Floating Hills.

We leave next week!

Better shoot, juicy fruit. ☺

Love,
Esme
xx

13

☆

2 February

☆ # *A nasty habit of spitting mucus* ☆

☆

Today we went to the Floating Hills!!!

Sometimes it's too cold for words here. During Alsun the average temperature is minus 30 degrees. I don't think you'd cope well, Mum, I know how much you love the heat. Near the Outlands it's even colder, so I had to get an extra toasty lining made for my suit.

'Now we must all be highly vigilant on this trip,' said Mrs Wobbleton from the stage in the assembly hall. 'It is essential that you follow the instructions the Space Cadets give you to the letter.'

At this point a pair of long antennae, followed by a rather large celestial body, proceeded to waddle up the stairs and onto the stage. He was dressed in a bulky white suit with more padding than several hundred packs of extra-large disposable nappies. How he moved was light years beyond my understanding.

'I am in charge of the Space Cadets who will be accompanying your group,' the suit said. 'Our mission is to keep you safe and return you to your parents in one piece. Now the trip today is without danger, providing the basic rules are adhered to.

'It will be a very long journey – a full fifteen minutes.' He paused, scanning the hall for effect. 'You must use this time to read through the safety instructions we will provide you.' With a nod of his head he finished and made his way back down the stairs, waddling towards the back of the hall.

I was not convinced he would be of much use if there *were* any problems. How on Kratos would he be able to help anybody in a crisis when he had the motion capacity of a dead marshmallow?

Either way, it was time to set off. Chattering excitedly, we shoved the safety instructions into our backpacks as soon as the Space Bus seats were introduced to our bums – Marshmallow Man's talk completely forgotten.

Stella sat next to Obi, and I sat next to Mars 15,122.

'You have much seen land this yet?' she asked.

'No, I haven't much seen land this… I mean I haven't seen much of this land yet.'

'My ancestor father's gatekeeper was city for the,' she said, beaming at me. 'My captain is father who the brought here you.'

Oh. My. Days.

Now I know how my English teacher at primary school felt when she went on and on at us for messing up our syntax. Not sure even *I* was this bad though.

I smiled at her, not wanting to hurt her feelings, then turned to the window to make like I was resting.

Mars took the hint and left me alone, fortunately, because if she hadn't I might have had to tell her to 'quiet be still hush lips your'.

Or something like that.

The journey was really interesting. The suns punctured chinks of light through the gloomy atmosphere so that every now and then I could see the sky. The ground was covered in dust and rock, just like in the sci-fi movies.

I counted sixteen craters, one of which was in the process of being converted into a new Swipsling stadium. We passed at least two canyons and what looked like a giant Walnut Whip, which Stella later told me was a dormant volcano.

The best was the nitrogen glaciers. They're so beautiful, the vapours appearing way before we reached them. The smoky mists rose up 103 metres, reaching out like a hungry person's hand for the sweets at a pick 'n' mix shop. Not just any pick 'n' mix either, but the kind that goes on for miles and miles and has so many sweets you need to spend at least an hour looking before making your choice. Like the one on our high street.

Just before our arrival we had to suffer the obligatory educational talk from the geography teacher, Mr Landmass. I glanced at Stella as he started, and both of us rolled our eyes.

'According to images and data collected by KASA's latest satellite readings, each of these hills measures three to five miles across,' he began. 'They border the Outlands as you are aware, just one of the reasons they are considered dangerous. The hills are in the vast area known as the Solar Plain.'

'Sir, I thought the captain said they weren't dangerous,' called one of the kids from the back. Mr Landmass completely ignored him.

'These hills, of which there are five in total, are suspended above a sea of frozen nitrogen, resulting in them drifting. However, they are stabilised by the huge blocks of nitrogen ice that stop them from drifting away completely.' He finally paused, looking around, hoping that the kids were as excited about this information as he was.

'They are a wonderful example of Kratos' rare and fascinating geological activity. Thus the reason for our visit – nowhere else in the entire known universe will you find such a place.'

Blah, blah, blah.

This was all very good and interesting, but I'd just made a devastating discovery.

I had a salad for lunch.

Again. ☹

Everybody knows salad isn't proper food. I don't know why Luna keeps giving it to me. Stella says she thinks it's because she wants me to 'experience contentment'.

I guess she wants me to feel at home, which is lovely, but in that case she ought to cook me fish finger sandwiches or beans on toast. When I suggested this, Stella was shocked. It took me ages to explain fish don't actually have fingers.

None of which alters the fact that salad is *literally*

ruining my life.

'Needless to say, once we arrive you must use your time well. Complete your worksheets. Our objective is to discover just how special the atmosphere and geological make-up of the Floating Hills is,' Mr Landmass continued. 'Who knows, one amongst you might one day be responsible for inventing a way to safely mine the hills of their precious metals. Now stay in your groups, no wandering off on your own. You must be careful to remain on the specially marked paths.' He started to wind down, just as we pulled up at the entrance to the Floating Hills pathway.

'Finally, if you do find any Greater Spotted Froids, don't touch them. They have a nasty habit of spitting mucus when feeling threatened, and may even bite. Simply take a photograph to include in your project folder.'

Climbing out of the Space Bus, we were greeted by a mass of nitrogen fog. Visibility was quite poor so everybody moved in single file along the path, walking as fast as we dared, tiny backpacks strapped to our backs.

Stella, Obi and me got to work on our sheets straight away, keen to get them finished. Mr Landmass warned us last week that if we didn't complete our sheets we would have to stay behind to clean the geography classroom for the rest of the month.

Which is why the next thing happened…

Love you lots, apricots. ☺

Esme

xx

14

2 February

☆ **Who's going in first?**

☆

☆

After 'lunch', during which I managed to persuade Mars to part with some of her Moon Cake – made of cheese, naturally – we went back out to complete our sheets. The three of us got ours done very quickly, so we could spend the rest of the afternoon exploring.

Shoving the completed sheets in our backpacks, we raced along the now-familiar path as fast as bats out of a cave at supper time, anxious to view the hills further up.

The path wound around the hill like a 150.3-metre wriggly snake, coiling around a large tree trunk. After a while it narrowed to the point where single file was our only option. This was followed by a steep incline, with fierce rocks on either side.

Up and up we climbed until, 37.6 metres from the top, we stopped to listen to the silence. This was promptly interrupted by an almighty scream coming from below.

Without saying a word we scrambled down as fast as possible. Close to the bottom we found Mars standing stock still, crying her eyes out.

'For what purpose are you troubled, Mars?' Stella asked, before Obi or me had recovered enough to even breathe at a normal rate, never mind think of a question.

'My away sheet blown has, into cave this here over,' she replied, in between her sniffles. 'My group lost I.'

Fortunately Stella, being an expert at decoding Mars' chatter, was able to work out what the problem was.

'Do not suffer alarm or trepidation, you will not experience conflict,' she said, placing her right arms around Mars' shoulders. 'We will inform Mr Landmass that you accomplished the completion of the sheet correctly. You will not receive a significant punishment.'

'Will yes I, hates me he.' Her bottom lip was quivering. Her tears were great big fat blobs of purple gunk. They ran down her face, landing on the ground, sending vapours sizzling skywards.

'Mr Landmass experiences deep discontent with everyone, you are not isolated in this,' said Stella.

'It's OK, we'll go into the cave to find it, don't worry,' volunteered Obi.

'No, we are unable to fulfil this notion, Obi. Our concise instructions were to remain on the designated pathways,' said Stella.

'I think we should go in,' I said. 'It's just a little way from the path, it's not like we'd be jumping off the side. And anyway, it's only a small cave from the looks of it.'

'Affirmative, I perfectly comprehend this dilemma. However, my father secured from me a guarantee I would be excessively vigilant.'

'I know, I was there, but nothing will happen to us,' I said. 'As long as we stick together. It's not like when your uncle came thirty years ago, we're much better protected now. The Space Cadets are with us just down the hill. If one of us doesn't return to the Space Bus they'll come and find us.'

'It will be fine, we'll just go into the cave, retrieve the sheet and then return to the path,' Obi joined in. 'OK, everybody?' Mars and me nodded in agreement, but Stella still seemed unhappy.

'If you're going to be Head Girl, you'll need to look after the students,' I said. 'You may as well start now. Anyway it's three against one, so you're outvoted.'

She looked at the three of us waiting expectantly, and after eight seconds caved in.

All four of us crept towards the mouth of the cave, each of us holding the next person in line.

'Who's going in first?' I asked, hoping someone would volunteer.

'Me not,' said Mars, shaking. 'Scared and fearful, I am.'

'I will precede anyone else, however you must make a solemn oath to pursue me, subsequent to my departure,' Stella said.

'Brilliant,' I said, faking a smile as she went ahead, followed by me, Obi and then Mars. The cave was as dark as Gran's food cupboard at midnight. This was not going to be as easy as it looked. But the darkness had never put me off of finding biscuits, so it sure as heck wasn't going to stop me finding this worksheet.

'I've changed my mind, I think we should go back,' said Obi.

'Negative, it is past the time of indecision. Arrival is imminent,' said Stella. 'We must proceed within the interior of the cave for three minutes. Then should we fail in our mission to locate and retrieve the sheet, we will retreat and resume our journey on designated pathway. Agreed?'

'Agreed,' we all said.

'Wait, I've got a brand new *Light Up Your World Power Torch* in my backpack,' said Obi.

He muddled around for what seemed like an age. You'd think having six arms would make it a quicker process. You'd be so wrong.

Finally after thirty-eight seconds he switched on the torch. We let out a gasp – the cave was so vast. It looked like it went on for miles. Tons of stalactites dripped from its ceiling, pointing at us like a thousand exclamation marks.

Which just goes to show, you shouldn't judge a book by its cover. Or a cave by its mouth.

The next few moments were spent poking around trying to find the stupid worksheet. Two minutes, thirteen seconds into our search a deep voice said, 'Is this what you're looking for?' I nearly jumped out of my custom-designed spacesuit skin!

A large figure shuffled into our field of vision,

waving a sheet of paper at us like a white flag. His face was a pasty smudge in the low light of the cave, his facial hair a vast furry mass.

He had two chains attached to his ankles, so that, by the time he'd walked 2.72 metres, it was clear he wouldn't be able reach us.

'Wh… who are you?' asked Stella, keeping two of her eyes on Mars, who looked like she was about to run and grab her worksheet.

'More to the point, who are *you*?' he asked. 'Have you come from the city? You are clearly not from the Outlands, you are too well-groomed.'

'Yes, we're on a day trip with our school,' I said. 'We've come in for the sheet, sir, please can you give it to us??'

'Yes, yes, here… take it,' he said, throwing it towards us.

'But, what exactly are you doing here?' Obi asked, finally finding his voice. 'And what is your name?'

'I'm forced to come into the caves every day to dig for the precious metals which are hidden beneath the surface of the Floating Hills,' he said. 'My name is Kepler.'

Obi gasped. I watched Stella as I took in the enormity of the moment. Her head jerked up. 'Kindly duplicate your response.'

'I said, my name is Kepler,' he repeated, looking at each of us in turn, confused at the reaction his name had provoked.

And then suddenly…

Everything.

Made.

Sense.

Gotta zip, apple pip. ☺

Esme

xx

15

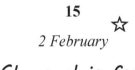

2 February

She real is for?

'You mean you're Kepler 45,092? *The* Kepler who went missing thirty years ago?' I asked. To the left of me Stella gasped, only managing to stay upright because Obi was propping her up.

'Why yes, how did you know this? Surely you are too young to have this information?' he asked, taking the opportunity to sit down on the nearest rock. 'Oh, and please call me Kep.'

'Only the whole of the planet has heard your story,' Obi said. 'The reason there have been no trips here for thirty years is because of your disappearance.'

'Well that explains why I've never seen anyone from Perihelion.' he said. 'I always hoped one day someone would come. I never dreamt an alien would find me, though.'

'Yes, it's a bit of a shock, but you will get used to it. I did,' I said brightly. Everyone swished round to look at me.

'She real is for?' asked Mars, cutting through the silence.

'Um… er… my name is Stella 12,614, daughter of Armstrong 6,209,' she said, waiting eleven seconds for the information to sink in before continuing, 'My deep comprehension is puzzled and confused. Please inform me truthfully, are you my Uncle Kep?'

'I… you… you're Armstrong's girl?' said Kep, astonishment and disbelief playing a game of tag on his face. 'Which makes you my niece?'

'Affirmative! My father will find it exceptionally difficult to comprehend this astonishing occurrence. I am scarcely able to believe it myself. We have an abundance of conversation to create,' she said.

Rushing forward, we attacked him with our questions. Finally he held up his hands to make us stop. Motioning for us to sit down, he began to tell us his story.

'I was captured when, like you and your alien, I moved away from the main path. I'd been walking with Armstrong when he spotted a light further up. It was a lot higher than we were permitted to go,' he said. 'Armstrong dared me to investigate so I climbed up, despite our friends telling me not to.'

After pausing for a moment, he continued. 'I was genuinely curious about the light, and there were rumours that precious metals were to be found in and around the rocks here. I wanted to take some back for my mother. I'd hoped she would think I was brave. Despite what she used to say to me, I always felt she favoured Armstrong.' He stopped, looking down. He sighed.

'I clambered up the hill, which got much steeper

than I'd expected. The atmosphere became denser nearer the top, with clouds of thick vapour swirling around, making it increasingly difficult for me to see. Before long I became disorientated.'

'That must have been so scary for you,' said Obi. 'Out here on your own.'

Kep nodded.

'I was just about to turn back when I spotted the source of the light – a lantern, hanging at the entrance of a small cave. This was the point when I should have turned back but, unable to contain my curiosity, I crept closer. Getting down on my hands and knees, I looked inside.'

He rubbed his knees as if what he was describing had just happened.

'Inside were two people chained up, both of them digging and scraping away at one of the walls. To the side of each of them was a small tray with shiny nuggets of precious metals, sparkling like golden stars in a midnight sky.'

He looked at us with such intensity. 'Those nuggets were the most beautiful things I'd *ever* seen. Anyone would have done the same,' he said, his eyes pleading with us to understand.

'They said they were Bad Ones, but were considered too weak to remain part of the central group. They'd been made to mine the hills, digging out the precious metals for years and years. I was urged to leave before I was caught, but I didn't listen.'

He shook his head, regret driving every word. 'I had my heart set on taking one of those nuggets home with me and nothing would distract me. Unfortunately I lingered in the cave for too long. Just as I was moving out, a great shadow fell upon me. It was the biggest Bad One that ever existed. Hubble. My fate was sealed.' He paused, and rubbed his temple. His harrowing experience had dug deep furrows across his face.

'I was taken to the main camp, some ten miles from the Floating Hills, where I stayed for four years. Since the age of sixteen I've been made to work. Digging within these caves on a daily basis, never seeing anyone. Moving once a week, from one hill to the next.'

He stopped and looked up, panic written across his face. 'You must go now. They will be coming for me within the hour. If they find you they will take you prisoner too.'

'It is imperative that you depart with us, Uncle Kep,' said Stella. 'Withdrawing without you is beyond consideration.'

'I cannot. If they find me missing they will know something is wrong and give chase – you won't leave these hills,' he replied anxiously. 'I couldn't have your imprisonment on my conscience.'

'But—'

'No, he's right,' said Obi. 'He can't come, but we can go back and tell others he's safe.'

'Yes, maybe they'll come back and get him,' I said.

'You *MUST* go,' Kep repeated, his eyes pleading with her to understand, 'otherwise history will repeat itself and you too will be trapped.'

'I consider this to be unacceptable, however I concede it is potentially the correct course of action at this precise moment,' she said. 'Please have confidence that a reappearance will occur and liberation will be within your grasp.'

'*Yes, yes, now go!*' he urged.

With the decision made, we hurried back down the hill to the Space Bus. We didn't tell anyone what we'd seen. It was obvious we'd get into big trouble for going off the path and it wasn't like anyone could do anything right then.

The last thing we wanted was a rescue attempt without the proper back-up. No, all everybody wanted was to get out of there as quickly as possible and tell Armstrong.

All the way home I struggled to contain my excitement. Stella kept nudging me, grinning so widely I thought her face would split in two. The journey seemed to take forever, much longer than on the way there. Finally the Space Bus pulled up into the school Jetcar park, where Armstrong was waiting.

'Father, you must maintain great composure at the news we are momentarily to impart.'

'Well, nice to see you too,' he said, pulling her into a hug. 'I'm just glad you're home and in one piece. I can't wait to hear about your day, but your mother is keen to hear too, so save it for when you're home.'

'But Father, we—'

'*Shooting stars*, Stella, it can wait for a few

minutes,' he said, walking around to the other side of the Jetcar. 'Jump in, girls.'

'We found Kep!' we both shouted, stopping him in his tracks.

'What did you say?'

'Kep, your brother. He was on one of the Floating Hills, working in a cave,' I said.

'This is true?' he asked, shaking his head in disbelief.

'Affirmative. We deviated away from the path…' She paused, looking at him apologetically. 'We did not deviate immensely, merely to assist a student who had mislaid her worksheet. She was experiencing enormous trauma.'

'We entered a cave and found Kep there,' I said. 'He told us the story of his capture.'

'Capture?'

'Affirmative. It is as we always feared. A Bad One called Hubble imprisoned him and has compelled him to work in the caves, digging for precious metals every day.'

'My poor, poor brother. How can he have deserved such a miserable fate?' he said, purple tears squelching down his face. He sat down on the front seat of the Jetcar, his shoulders shaking.

'I don't know if I'm crying with sadness at his fate, or happiness that he is alive.' He turned to face us, by now seated behind him. 'One thing is certain, girls, I will leave no stone unturned until I get my brother back to Perihelion, where he belongs.'

'Can we come with you?'

'Affirmative, Father, it is essential that we accompany you on the rescue mission. It is only Esme and I who are fully aware of the whereabouts of the cave,' Stella said hopefully.

'No, I will not put you in any more danger. I'll speak to my friends in government, who will no doubt provide me with an armed guard to rescue him,' he said forcefully. 'You will show us his location on a map.'

'But we need to come! If we don't you'll never find him!' I argued.

'Esme articulates with great precision. Certainly, we may pinpoint the exact hill. However, to ascertain the entrance to the cave will be problematic without our presence.'

'I understand your point, but I still don't approve. You can discuss it with Luna once you get home. She can decide. But don't expect her to agree either.'

Better go, pizza dough. ☹

Love,

Esme

xx

16

4 February

We're going back

That. Is. All.

17

7 February

☆ We've been expecting you ☆

What a week! Sorry I haven't posted a blog for a while, it's just that I've had the craziest few days of my entire life. Well, apart from when I first arrived on Kratos.

Stella and me knew where Kep was so we were allowed to go with the rescue party to show them 'the spot'. It was a much quicker journey this time, because we weren't travelling with a whole bunch of kids. Plus our transport was a speedier vehicle, properly kitted out with a mega-strength engine, bumpers and lights.

We both felt a mixture of excitement and fear. Those rumours about the Bad Ones were even more worrying now there was a real possibility we might come across some.

The fiercest bunch of soldiers on the planet came with us – the Thunderbusters. Luna had only agreed to let us go providing we were accompanied by them.

'It's important we stay together,' said General

Swett, their commander, sounding more British than the Royal Family. 'We want each and every one of us to return safe and well. Hopefully we will have an extra one with us for the journey back.'

'Yes, we *must* bring my brother back,' said Armstrong.

'Do not become agitated, Father,' Stella said. 'We will locate him once again, and on this occasion I remain convinced we will be successful in liberating him.'

'I just wish your grandmother was here, she would have been overjoyed. She died not knowing whether he was dead or alive,' he sighed.

'Come along, let's get to it,' said the general, as our group stepped onto the now familiar hill. Kep had told us that they rotated the hills he worked on, staying on one for a week, before being moved to another. Because our last visit was so recent, we guessed he was probably on the same hill as before. Moving up the hill as fast as we could, we found the entrance to the cave in no time at all.

'You are sure this is it?' asked the general.

'Affirmative. This is definitely the precise one,' said Stella.

With hope in our hearts we crept in, but once our eyes had adjusted to the dark it was obvious Kep wasn't there. Armstrong sat down, his antennae drooping forlornly.

The decision was made to push on up the hill to investigate further. Within three minutes and forty-seven seconds there came a sharp noise to our right.

Catching our eyes, the general brought his finger up to his lips. Everyone nodded at him.

Letting the general take the lead, we crept towards the sound, arriving at the new cave entrance in forty-four seconds.

Success!

As soon as he spotted him, Armstrong forgot everything and rushed into the cave. He grabbed Kep up into the biggest hug, squishing him like someone trying to get the last note out of an accordion.

Once Kep had got over the surprise of a sudden 'death by hugging' attack from the brother he hadn't seen in thirty years, he grabbed the general's hand and urged him to get us out of the area.

'They know I have spoken to the children. I had to tell them, they saw their footprints on the cave floor,' he said. 'They've put extra guards on the hills ever since.'

'Well, we're not leaving without you,' said the general. 'Lieutenant Cosmos, the *Cyclops Laser* please.'

His second-in-command opened the bag he'd been carrying and removed a humungous laser. He pointed it at the thick chains around Kep's leg. A zap of light later and Kep was free.

Except he wasn't.

Because at that exact moment three new visitors arrived.

In the entrance stood the biggest alien I'd ever seen, flanked by two smaller ones. He had one arm missing and patches over two of his eyes. A scar snaked its way down his cheek, zigzagging like a zip until it reached his mouth where it was met by a missing top lip and a line of jagged teeth.

He looked like his favourite meal might be toddler on toast.

'*Welcome*,' he boomed, so loudly we all jumped. Stella moved behind Armstrong for protection, while I moved behind the nearest Space Cadet. My heart thudded ferociously, my stomach clenched into a tight knot.

Peeking around the side to get a better look, I saw Kep edging himself towards the wall, his eyes lowered.

'We've been expecting you and are honoured by your presence. It appears you have some notion of removing Mr Kep here,' said The Face.

'You have no right to do this,' Armstrong insisted, a single line of sweat trickling down the side of his face. 'Keeping him is unjust, I—'

'Just like the injustice I experienced many moons ago at the hands of your father.'

'What? Who are you?' asked General Swett.

'My name is Hubble 12,416. The one who was falsely banished thirty-three years ago by their father,' he said in his best toxic accent, nodding his head towards Kep and then Armstrong.

Armstrong's eyes widened in recognition. '*Shooting stars!* Hubble 12,416? *The* Hubble who kept stowing away on early spaceship missions to Earth?' he asked in disbelief.

'One and the same,' Hubble replied, a sneer

covering his gigantic mushroom of a face.

'So you kidnapped Kep to get revenge?' the general asked.

'You could say that. It's certainly brought me a lot of pleasure keeping Kep this way. Indeed it was a happy accident the day we found him.'

'But for what purpose did you detain Kep? He was simply an innocent boy,' Stella asked, stepping out from behind her dad.

'*So was I*,' Hubble bellowed, making us jump again.

'You were found guilty of trespassing on government property six times,' Armstrong said, trying to reason with him. 'The last time you got onto a spaceship you hid so well the crew didn't find you until they'd landed on Earth. You nearly exposed us to two humans who were in the vicinity.

'You could have ruined years and years of carefully concealed missions. Then, when the mission returned, you tried to steal the music box they'd brought back. You were guilty as charged, Hubble.'

'The facts are undeniable, but you fail to understand the purpose. I wanted to prove that someone from a lower order could make a successful mission to Earth. People like us were never given a chance. The music box was just an impetuous youthful mistake. I am not a thief and I did not deserve to be banished.'

'Your fate was sealed the moment you walked onto a spaceship without official permission, regardless of your reasons,' the general said. 'You had no business being there. You have only yourself to blame.'

'And *YOUR* fate was sealed the moment *YOU* walked into this cave! *YOU* have no business stepping foot onto the Floating Hills,' Hubble boomed. 'They are close to the Outlands, which makes them our territory! *YOU* only have *YOURSELF* to blame for Kep being taken prisoner! And for what's about to happen!'

I was desperate to ask him why he was booming so much and why he was using lots of exclamation marks in his speech, but figured now wasn't a good time.

And anyway, while I was hiding behind a Space Cadet, I'd had the beginning of an idea going round my head. I just had to wait for the right moment...

Major rush, candy crush. ☺

Love,

Esme

xx

18

7 February

Muuurrrgghhh, it talked to me

'Now look here, we are not responsible for your banishment,' said the general. 'Even if you were sent here unfairly, you simply cannot blame these two. Now we are asking you to let us go. It's the decent thing to do.'

'Well, now, I think you might have a point,' said Hubble, rubbing his chin. 'Therefore, I choose to release you.'

'Really?' said Armstrong.

'No. Not really,' he said, a mean grin slapped back across his face.

Now he was beginning to annoy me. It was obvious that Hubble was one angry alien, with a lot of unresolved issues, but there was no need to be quite so sarcastic.

'It may be the decent thing to do, but you forget – I'm not decent. Therefore, you will become my servants, aside from Armstrong, who will be brought to these hills to toil alongside his brother every day.

'And don't even think about trying to escape,' he said. 'I have fifty of my men and women outside, waiting to guide you back to our settlement. My gun is fully loaded and keen to make your acquaintance.'

He paused, looking around the cave. 'Your soldiers won't stand a chance, so tell them to go back to Perihelion immediately.'

The general turned and shrugged an apology to Armstrong. I couldn't believe he'd given up so easily. He switched on his radio and began waffling into it.

While everyone was distracted with the general, I focused on getting Stella's attention, tugging at her suit. She inched towards me, a look of deep sadness on her face.

I motioned with my head a plan to hide behind a crag. It wasn't a big area, but it was enough to provide me with a decent hiding place. She nodded and winked. I didn't want to leave them, but someone had to go back to Perihelion and tell people what had happened.

She flicked her eyes over one of Hubble's men, whose jacket flipped up and over his head. He cried out in surprise, diverting attention, allowing me enough time to scramble into the space conveniently provided by the cave's interior design. I snuggled as close to the wall as I could, not knowing how long it'd be before they left.

It was at this point that my attention was distracted by something so brilliant I couldn't believe my eyes. I was staring at the ledge on the wall next to my head when I realised there was something staring right back at me – a Greater Spotted Froid. It looked a bit like a frog, but had seven legs and its red skin was covered in yellow spots.

I couldn't resist getting closer, so I leaned across until my helmet nearly touched its 9mm nose. It didn't move away, just sat there blinking and gulping, until finally it spat at me and jumped off the ledge, leaving me covered with a whole load of gunge dripping down my spacesuit. Who knew something so little could produce so much goo?

Then something really tricky happened.

It was slow to begin with. I could feel a kind of crescendo building until it reached a peak. It turned first my nose and then my whole face into a contorted mass of itchy discomfort, the eruption within held back only by sheer willpower.

The general, having finished giving his instructions to his men, left only one course of action for the captors.

'Seize them all,' said Hubble, turning and walking towards the entrance of the cave as his guards grabbed the group.

At which precise moment.

I.

Sneezed.

Hubble turned round in the blink of several eyes.

'What was that?' he asked.

'Oh, nothing,' said Stella.

'That was *not* nothing,' Hubble said, his eyes darting across the cave. 'And that noise didn't come from anyone here,' he continued, snaking his way through our group.

'The last time I heard that sound was thirty-three years ago, when I was on Planet Earth. The damp conditions of certain countries – such as England – cause its inhabitants to develop infections not experienced by our species but known to them as "colds".

'They bring on symptoms such as coughing and sneezing, which is the noise you heard. Sometimes the humans develop a strange desire to put their fingers up their nose, but when they do some of their brain cells fall out. It is not a life-threatening illness for the inhabitants of Earth, but to us it can be fatal if we are not inoculated.' He paused for effect, looking round at his men. 'And *nobody* in the Outlands is inoculated.'

Apart from the not-so-actual-fact about brain cell leakage, plus no mention of snot or bogies, I was quite impressed with his knowledge of colds.

'OK, you got me,' I said, holding my hands up as I moved out from my hiding place. I figured there was little point in trying to hide any longer.

Hubble and his crew of bad guys stared at me in alarm. Finally one of the guards broke the silence. 'What is this small creature?'

'My name is Esme, and I *am* here, thank you very much, so you can jolly well ask me yourself.'

'Muuurrrgghhh, it talked to me,' the guard exclaimed in horror, backing off much quicker than was safe in such a confined space.

'Calm down,' said another guard. 'It's more scared

of you than you are of it. It won't hurt you.'

'I object to being called 'it', so I *will* hurt you if you don't improve your manners,' I said.

'Indeed this creature, which is called a human, has great potential to harm us. If it has a cold we could contract it and become ill very quickly,' Hubble informed his guards.

'Yes, that's right, you'd better go now. I can feel another sneeze coming on, and I think you should know that my nose contains the most ridiculously violent, extra-spreadable snot! Why, I used to win all the snot-flinging competitions in our street when I was younger,' I said, faking a cough while I was at it, winking at Stella and Armstrong as I doubled over, acting out a fit.

'Affirmative, furthermore the entire company has experienced exceedingly close proximity to Esme for a significant number of days,' said Stella. 'It is apparent to everyone present that you have no alternative but to liberate us, otherwise you place yourself and your men in grave jeopardy.'

'She's right,' said Hubble. 'All of us need to get away from them. We can't take any chances on taking this back to the settlement, it would destroy us if an infection spread.'

Armstrong sneezed over Kep, then walked towards Hubble. At which point the Bad Ones evacuated the cave. So much for Hubble's brave talk. Scared off by one of the tiniest organisms to have ever lived – bacteria.

Rushing to the cave entrance we were relieved

to see they'd already got to the bottom of the hill. Hubble turned around for one last look, raised his right fists at us and growled something or other about not being finished with us yet, before finally disappearing.

All of which left us free to climb down the hill and make our way to our vehicle. Thankfully the Thunderbusters hadn't listened to their commander, deciding to wait for another hour. So we got home safely *and* with a new member to add to the family.

By the way, just so you know, I don't have a cold or anything, although I definitely have an allergy to Greater Spotted Froids. I'm pretty sure some of its gunk got into my suit and irritated my nose. You do *not* want to know what happens to the inside of a spacesuit when you sneeze…

Grim.

Still, as Gran used to say – 'all's well that ends well'.

Feeling ace, cherry lace. ☺

Love,

Esme

xx

19

12 February

I will experience extreme disrespect

'Your comprehension should be great in understanding the negative emotions which arise through unpopularity at school,' Stella growled at me. 'I am convinced that you pledged to assist me in gaining additional votes for the Head Girl election!'

She's been getting upset because she's still not making inroads into that precious place commonly known as the *Peer Acceptance Zone*. I *do* understand how she feels, but there really is no need to take it out on me.

'You're not exactly helping much, are you?' I was hurt by her words. 'I've seen more enthusiasm in a dead Greater Spotted Froid!'

'But you stated categorically you would promote me, to ensure my popularity throughout the school. This has not materialised, Esme. Therefore, I must conclude that you made an insincere claim.'

'Well pardon me for neglecting to bring my *How to Win Friends and Influence Aliens* book.'

I slammed out of the room, stomped to the stairs, before bursting into tears.

The door opened forty-three seconds later. She came and sat next to me. 'I apologise profusely. It is difficult to comprehend I will not gain votes for this election. My father will be most displeased.' She was genuinely worried he'd be cross with her if she didn't win.

'I will experience maximum disrespect for a significant length of time. I am deeply distressed to discover that the campaign posters have been destroyed. Some have been removed and used for propelling knives at.'

Mum, I tried to comfort her, but it was no use, she wasn't having any of it. She wouldn't even cheer up when I told her that she'd get heaps of kudos for being part of Kep's rescue party. She looked horrified – she thought 'kudos' was some kind of nasty bug.

Returning to school, I put extra effort into organising the election campaign. In my short time as her manager I've doubled her supporters. Admittedly this is only one extra vote, but still… it's a start.

Obi and me have been putting up posters everywhere, including the girls' toilets. But these aliens are excellent at art. They've used their talents to destroy the posters. There are moustaches, extra antennae and one numpty has even turned her into a boy by drawing some boy's front bottom bits, aka willy, on her.

Rude. ☹

It's obvious that we're going to need something

miraculous to make Stella popular.

The ear-piercing idea was officially a failure. Having me as her best friend has helped a bit. She does get invited to more parties now, but in truth this is mainly because everyone knows I won't go anywhere without her.

I've tried to help her, telling her to let other people answer the questions first in class, but she doesn't listen. She's not doing it to be top dog. She just loves learning and enjoys discussing things with the teachers.

What to do now…?

*

Kep has struggled with the changes that have taken place in Perihelion since he's been gone. He's bewildered by the house, not to mention the new gadgets within it. The TV, in particular, turns him into a zombie – he just sits and stares at it, not talking to anyone all day, pausing just to eat. Come to think of it, not much different to a lot of people on Earth…

He's gone into a state of shock since Armstrong took him out shopping. The variety of goods on sale has blown his mind, and he can't believe the price rises. Jetcars have improved dramatically while he was in captivity *and* the Swipsling has been invented.

I wonder if the same thing would happen to me if I ever came back to Earth. Would the changes be so vast I'd struggle to cope?

He's taken to sitting in the corner of the room, reading Luna's *Gigantic Book of Inspirational But*

Ridiculously Cheesy Quotes. I think it's giving him some kind of comfort. He certainly seems happiest when left alone.

Armstrong says he's just processing stuff, that he was always the more thoughtful of the two of them. Given time, he'll adjust.

He's having an official Welcome Home Ceremony soon, which is brilliant. I'm properly worried about how Kep will cope though. He's to give a speech, which will be difficult as he doesn't really talk to anyone outside of the family unless it's to say stuff like, 'When you start seeing your worth, you'll find it harder to stay around those who don't' – to the postman. And, 'Let your smile change the world, don't let the world change your smile' – to the owner of Lord of the Wings.

They know his story so they nod politely, shake his hands, clap him on the back and don't let on that he's acting weird. I'm worried about how others will respond though.

I know he's anxious about what the future holds, because he isn't trained to do any job that will earn him decent Orbits.

He doesn't want to be a burden on the family. Rather, he wants to make his own way in life. Armstrong is doing his best to get him a job.

He's contacted everyone he knows, but, aside from dressing as a chicken to promote Lord of the Wings for the day, nothing's come up yet.

He can't go to university as you aren't allowed to go over the age of thirty here, they think you're too old. For such an advanced society they sure are behind with some things.

But don't worry, I think I've got it sorted. I'd been helping him put together a speech for the ceremony when I had this sudden moment of genius, one that might just put Kep back on the 'I've got a job and am on the road to recovery' map.

I've definitely overdone the excitement factor this year, so it's been good to have a few days of routine, experience a bit of normality. Well, as much can be expected, living on a planet billions of light years away from Earth.

I think about you all a lot. I hope Isaac's finally decided what he wants to be when he grows up. The last time I spoke to him he wanted to be a trumpet. Given the noise that comes out of his bum, I think it's probably a sound choice.

I hope Maisie's not having nightmares any more. If she is, you can give her the lamp from my bedroom. She always wanted it.

Give them both a big hug from me.

Gotta fly, cherry pie. ☺

Love you!

Esme

xxx

20

16 February

You're welcome

Stella and me were invited to sit on the stage at Kep's Welcome Home Ceremony. As I climbed the stairs I spotted Rodney Swineheart making his way onto the opposite side of the stage.

I made a hasty retreat, and sat down next to Armstrong and Luna instead. Stella followed so swiftly she got there before me. I still haven't got over being made to feel stupid by Rodney when I went on his ridiculous show. He's the most patronising alien I've ever met.

He was busy showing off to some girls who had come to the front of the hall. As he chatted, he flexed the muscles on his three right arms, showing off his tattoos. One of which looked familiar.

'There's that tattoo again,' I said.

'It's nothing to worry about,' said Armstrong, before Stella had a chance to respond. 'It's just a symbol which has been adopted by a secret society that has plans to take over Planet Earth, killing all known life before moving us Kratons to live there forever.'

'*Whaaaaaaaaaaaaaaat?* Are you serious? Please tell me you're not?' I asked, blood draining from every part of my body and heading south at a ridiculously unhealthy pace.

'Armstrong, don't scare the girl,' said Luna, her four eyes and eyebrows working overtime in mock exasperation.

'Your face is a picture,' said Armstrong. 'Only joking! Why would we do that? You humans are a wonderful race, so full of kindness to each other and the world around you,' he continued. 'Besides, Kratos is wonderful, why would we want to leave?' Luna nudged him as Mrs Wobbleton approached in a blue dress so loud I needed earplugs.

'Good evening, Armstrong, Luna, Stella, Esme,' she said, nodding her head with each name. 'I wonder if I might have a quiet word with you afterwards, please?' Giving Luna and Armstrong a meaningful look, she strode towards her seat on the stage, her dress introducing itself to everyone along the way.

The ceremony wasn't much different to Markham High's end of year award bash. There were even some 'musical' moments, where students attempted to play instruments.

It was chaos because the two violinists were so star-struck over Rodney Swincheart that they just sat there with their mouths open. Didn't take their eyes off of him, even when they were playing.

Facing in the wrong direction, their bows did untold damage to the oboe player's neck and back, before finally moving on to his ears. This erupted into a fight, only stopped when Mrs Wobbleton took the mic, harpooning them with her voice, 'Desist. Immediately!' Which of course they did.

I wouldn't want to be in their shoes on Monday morning...

Finally the 'music', relieved of its duties, stopped. There was a hush across the hall as Mrs Grinchbum, the school governor, walked across the stage to the podium, her frizzy hair flowing behind her like a bunch of traumatised question marks.

Everyone had heard the news about Kep's return, but apart from the family, a close friend and the postman, nobody had actually seen him. Kep's old school friends sat at the front of the hall with us. Great expectations sat everywhere else.

Mrs Grinchbum cleared her throat before smiling at everybody like she was the Queen. 'Welcome, Ladies and Gentlemen. It is with enormous pleasure I welcome you to our Welcome Home Ceremony for Kepler 45,092,' she said, her voice sounding like a handful of nails being scratched up and down a blackboard. 'Let's welcome him together as he joins us onstage tonight. Welcome,' she continued as he approached the stage.

'Somebody should tell her it's considered bad form to repeat the same word again and again in the same paragraph,' I whispered to Stella.

'You may potentially partake of this task,' she said.

'My pleasure.'

'Thank you.'

'You're welcome!' At which point we both fell about laughing.

'Shhhhh,' said Luna. 'We're getting to the important part now.'

Kep unfolded his sheet of paper as he walked across the stage. Everyone rose out of their seats, clapping and cheering like crazy.

'Thank you everybody,' Kep said, reading the first part of his pre-prepared speech. 'I dreamt of returning so many times. It's what kept me going all those years…'

His four eyes glistened as he spoke. But then he did the unexpected, crumpling up the piece of paper and placing it into his pocket. 'When life shuts a door… open it again. It's a door. That's how they work.'

'Yessss!' somebody shouted from the back.

Stella, Luna and Armstrong slid lower into their seats, hands joined in emotional unity. *I*, however, sat bolt upright, as I knew exactly what Kep was doing. It was all part of *The Plan*.

'Wear your tragedies as armour, not shackles. Remember, today is the day you worried about yesterday. I'm imperfect and yet my imperfections, like any great work of art, are what make me a masterpiece. Nothing is impossible. Why, the word itself says 'I'm possible'. By being yourself, you put something wonderful in the world that wasn't there before.'

'Preach it,' someone shouted, causing Kep to pause and grin.

'Mistakes are proof that you are trying. Altitude is determined by attitude. Never give up. Success is 1% inspiration, 99% perspiration. Be nice. The end.'

He nodded, put his three right hands up, and walked off stage. The audience was so moved, they were on their feet clapping and crying the instant he stopped.

The ceremony over, we mingled and ate tons of cake. Rodney Swineheart was in one corner talking to a very animated Kep for ages. Mrs Wobbleton, having circled the room a number of times, gestured for Luna and Armstrong to join her. Which they promptly did. When The Wobbleton calls, few dare resist.

I watched them disappear into a corner of the hall. They looked over at me several times, before resuming their chat. While Armstrong tapped his chin, Luna looked like she was crying. I nearly went over, but didn't think I'd be very useful and anyway they'd made it obvious they didn't want me around.

The Plan worked though! Rodney Swineheart offered Kep a five-minute spot to close the show, sharing his words of wisdom with the planet. *And* he's being paid enough Orbits to be able to move into his own house. The family have insisted that he stays for a bit longer though, so that they can keep their eyes on him.

Luna and Armstrong were muttering on the way home. I heard them mention Stella's name a couple of times, and they kept glancing back at me. I'm still wondering what's going on, no one will tell me anything. If Stella knows she's doing a good job of hiding it.

During my time away it's become apparent to me that grown-ups are complicated, no matter what planet they come from.

Fact.

Later maybe, jelly baby. ☺

Love,

Esme

xxx

21

20 February

Nobody situates Stella in the corner

Walking into school it was clear that the Head Boy and Girl election was all anybody could focus on. Hardly surprising considering that everyone was due to vote that day.

Yesterday I'd gone round and covered the defaced posters with new ones, but was gutted to see some of them had either been ripped down or drawn on again. I didn't, and still don't, understand why they're being like this. After all, Stella did play a big part in rescuing Kep. It seems they'll never like her no matter what she does.

At lunchtime the candidates were given five minutes each in the dining hall to explain to the school what they would bring to the role.

I'd written Stella's speech the night before and we'd practised for several hours. She wanted to pull out, but her dad would hear nothing of it. 'I was Head Boy *and* your grandmother was Head Girl,' he said. 'It's unthinkable you should *not* be Head Girl.'

No pressure then.

The usual bustle of the dining hall was replaced by a hush I hadn't heard since our last Christmas Eve together, Mum. That is, once we'd got Maisie and Isaac to bed.

It didn't last long, though, as the first candidate soon got to his feet to speak.

'I, Mario Pepperoni 1… er…' he started, '… would like to offer myself for the role of Head Boy. I am an ideal candidate as my father told me I am and he's always right about most things…' Stella told me he'd been named after a pizza delivery man who had introduced his father to the earthly delights of Italian food.

Of course, everybody was laughing, and there was no way to bounce back from that one. He couldn't get a word in edgeways so reluctantly gave up the stage to the next person.

Before long it was Stella's turn. For someone usually so confident, she was surprisingly nervous. The Stella who had stood up to Hubble was missing. In her place was a bowl of apple jelly which had got caught up in an earthquake.

'My gratitude is immense. Thank you to everyone for granting me permission to communicate with you today,' she said. 'I perfectly comprehend I am not the premier selection for the role of Head Girl. However, I would be filled with an abundance of gratitude for the opportunity to represent the students at this school.'

'Nobody wants you to represent us!' someone at

the back shouted. Others murmured in agreement.

'Why are you even giving a speech? You know they're going to fix it for you to win,' another called.

She looked at me in confusion, then putting her brave face on, she jutted out her chin. 'I do not possess knowledge of this information. However, if I am successfully elected I will pay close attention to your grievances and ensure the school has the greatest progression, facilitating the transformations you are eager to acquire.'

They let her continue with the speech, but didn't clap when she was finished. As we were leaving the hall, Mrs Wobbleton beckoned her into the headteacher's office.

Six minutes and twenty-one seconds later Stella emerged with purple eyes.

'What's she been saying to you?'

'She has informed me that my success in the election is assured, and told me not to become anxious.'

'There you go. So why are you upset?'

'You do not comprehend my dilemma. She has 'persuaded' a large number of students to vote for me, plus she's acquired the guaranteed support of the teaching staff. This is not a democratic election. I remain convinced it is a corrupt way to proceed.'

I put my arm around her as she began to cry again.

'The most abhorrent thing is that I remain unable to convince her of the mistaken nature of her actions. She has minimal comprehension of the reasons for my deep distress,' she continued.

'She has insisted I am triumphant in the election as she maintains an extreme obsession with my gift for repositioning things with my mind. I have also discovered she has conversed with my father and he is fully aware of this situation.'

I was gobsmacked. I knew it was important to Armstrong that she won, but I didn't think he'd agree to her success by allowing her to cheat. No wonder everyone hates Stella. I wondered if this had occurred to her.

'No wonder everybody has a deep hatred of me at this moment in time,' she said. 'I have been informed that my options are limited – I must remain committed to this success, and consider my family, not merely myself.'

'This is such an awful situation,' I said. Then, in a flash of inspiration, I grabbed her. 'Stella, what do you think is more important – winning the election or getting new friends at school, people who deeply respect you?' I asked.

'Honesty is of greater importance to me than either of these. Since our acquaintance I've become educated about the importance of maintaining an incorruptible attitude at all times,' she replied.

'Well, what would you say if you could be honest and, in doing so, gain the respect of the students at school?'

'Clarify this mystery – what strategies are you devising, Esme?'

So I filled her in.

She looked thoughtful for twelve seconds, before

replying, with a wide grin, 'Nobody situates Stella in the corner.' She'd tried on my idea for size and liked the fit.

Stella was buzzing with excitement as we waited to hear the election results. Mrs Wobbleton took to the stage and announced the new Head Boy first – Davidstar 2,993. He was a popular student who was bright, and shone in all his classes.

I don't think anyone was surprised that Pizza Boy hadn't been voted in.

Apart from his dad.

The inevitable announcement was made – Stella was officially Head Girl. The poor runner-up – Galaxy 21,302 – was devastated. I was surprised she even thought she'd stood a chance.

The slow, sarcastic clapping Stella received was punctuated with a full-stop when she rose to take the microphone from the headteacher.

'I would like to express my gratitude to those who voted for me,' she began. 'However, this would be a great deceit, as I am conscious the majority of you experienced extreme pressure to vote for me.'

Mrs Wobbleton gasped. The students were dumbstruck. You could have heard a tapestry pin drop.

'I officially resign from the position. As of now,' she continued. 'It is unacceptable to gain any position of power where coercion has occurred, therefore I *cannot* and *will not* be Head Girl of this school.'

She paused to look around the hall. 'I surrender my Head Girl position to Galaxy 21,302,' she said. 'Had the election not been manipulated, she would have won this election. It is the rightful outcome, and the only one my conscience will permit.'

Mrs Wobbleton's jaw was a see-saw, going up and down, up and down. I think she trapped some fluff in it at one point, but she was too busy flabbergasting to notice.

Then something amazing happened. The whole school – including the teachers – got to their feet and clapped like clapping was going out of fashion and they needed to get as much in as possible before it became completely extinct.

Galaxy was overwhelmed and ran to thank Stella, who was pretty overcome with emotion herself. I don't think she'll ever be unpopular again, with the students at least. Her dad and Mrs Wobbleton? Well, they're a different matter altogether.

It just goes to show – doing the right thing is always the right thing to do, especially if it really is the right thing to do.

Or something like that.

Armstrong's given me the next two days off of school. He says it's for the best, to keep out of The Wobbleton's way. I'm starting to miss you more and more. I miss the chocolate too. All this talk about Galaxy has given me the munchies, and the chocolate here's still rubbish.

I'll write again real soon.

Hitting the hay, Milky Way. ☺

Love,

Esme

xxx

22

23 February

Bra wars

Armstrong and Luna have grounded us just because we missed one piece of homework this week! After all we've just been through, they're going on about homework? Trust me to end up on a planet which has the same ideas about education as Earth.

'Every day may not be good, but there is always something good in every day,' said Kep.

'You're not helping, Kep, you're not the one grounded,' I said.

'Well, you must remember this – our greatest glory isn't in never falling, but rising every time we do,' he continued, nodding his head far too often to be taken seriously.

'Whatever.'

'OK, Esme, just trying to help.'

Obi came round just as Stella and me were having an argument about my 'maximum disrespectful manner' towards Kep. He called it 'Bra Wars', making Stella blush a dark shade of blue and me roll on the floor laughing. That did the trick. Soon we were friends again, and of course I apologised to Kep.

I've not told you this yet, Mum, but I've started to wish I was at home. I've been homesick for a while. I can't shake it off.

I told Stella and she offered to take me to the Planet Earth Exhibition again, which was nice, but right now all I want to do is see you, Maisie and Isaac. Even the stupid stuff – the stuff which used to drive me mad – seems OK now.

I bet Maisie's growing up fast. I hope she's got over the appendix operation she had two weeks before I left. I remember when she had her stitches removed, there was a catheter in her tummy sticking up. She looked down and said, 'Goodbye appendix, hello willy!' I can't think of her without remembering that. She's so funny.

I want you to know I've forgiven Isaac for messing up Gran's funeral last summer by singing 'Happy Birthday' at the top of his voice when the priest lit the candles.

I know he was only three at the time, so he couldn't be expected to understand. I get that now. I'm really sorry I lost my temper with him. Those two kids are the best little brother and sister anyone could ever ask for.

I'm sorry I was such a massive pain at times. I don't think I appreciated how much you did for us. I used to get properly annoyed at the people you had around all the time, but looking back now I can see how I wasn't much company for you. You must have found it hard bringing us up on your own.

I wish I knew what you were all doing…

I still like it here, the family are lovely to me, but I cannot believe I've come so far away from home to end up in a place with people who think grounding me is a good form of punishment. At least when you grounded me you had an actual reason for it, like when I tried to flush Maisie's Barbie collection down the loo.

Stella's just been in and told me we're going back for another visit to the Planet Earth Exhibition at the weekend. It's finished, ready for action and we've got tickets to go in a couple of days, before the official opening day! Apparently Armstrong has a big surprise for me. I love that they're trying to cheer me up. They really do care.

It'll be good to take Kep this time, to see his reaction to the different discoveries about Earth that have been made while he was away. He's always asking me questions about home and now he'll get to see some of the stuff we've talked about, even if it *is* displayed in a weird way.

I hope you're OK. Sorry I missed Isaac's fourth birthday.

Missing home, honeycomb. ☹

Love you lots,

Esme

xxxx

23

27 February

Because they don't know how to cook

Out of the corner of my eye I noticed Luna staring at me. We were getting ready to go to the Planet Earth Exhibition, the usual chaos of everyone scrambling for coats and shoes in the hall.

She can sometimes make a fuss when we're going out, but this time she seemed extra bothered. I thought she was going to tell me my new mega-heeled space boots weren't 'suitable attire', but she didn't say a word.

As we were leaving she gave everyone their usual hug, but when she got to me she grabbed and hugged me to near suffocation. That should have set the alarm bells ringing, but nope, little old trusting me just shoved it to the back of my mind and set off.

Within thirty-one seconds of arriving at the centre, Armstrong disappeared, so Stella and me wandered around with Kep. We'd got as far as the English Farm area and I was just explaining each animal to Kep when a stressed Armstrong reappeared with Sputnik.

They joined us as we moved over to the new zone – Human Fashion. It's now my favourite, but for all the wrong reasons. I don't know which decades they've been visiting but it looks like they've taken a whole heap of clothes from the last hundred years, thrown them up in the air and then dressed the mannequins in the order in which they landed.

There's a man wearing skin-tight gold hot pants, a T-shirt and a bow tie. He's got something that looks like a seatbelt across his chest and wrapped around his waist. Next to this exhibit is a woman wearing a pair of trainers, a long skirt and dinner jacket.

Oh, and a kilt.

On.

Her.

Head.

'Humans don't dress like this at all,' I said, rolling my eyes.

'Often finding meaning is not about doing things differently – it's about seeing things in different ways,' offered Kep, smiling as everyone gawped at him.

'Hasn't anyone ever taken a photo of humans wearing different outfits, to make sure they get this right? Has anyone actually spoken about fashion to the STAR students who've visited Earth?'

'Why, no, I don't believe anyone has,' said Sputnik. 'I'll make a note of that for the next mission. Yes, yes, excellent idea.'

Unbelievable.

'Come, come, follow me.' Sputnik beckoned.

'I'd like to introduce you to the new and best exhibit so far.'

We followed him down the long corridor, turning left, then left again, one more left turn and then a final left before coming to a standstill. At this point I thought there was nothing right about this place.

'Look, observe and be impressed,' said Sputnik. 'I give you… Africa!'

Oh boy, I *was* excited now, I've always wanted to visit Kenya! It did feel a little strange doing it in outer space, but beggars can't be choosers.

The animals in the safari zone were amazing. Two lions, four cheetahs and two leopards. They even had three elephants! Further in was an area with three hippos wallowing around in a huge slimy pond. While everybody was busy looking, an animal joke came to mind. I was giggling to myself when Sputnik stopped and glared at me.

'Esme, is this area not pleasing to you?' he asked, his face crumpled up like a warthog's backside.

'Oh no, it's wonderful. I was just thinking about something,' I giggled. 'Do you know why lions eat their meat raw?' I asked.

'No, I don't. Do you know why?' asked Sputnik, curiosity piqued.

'It's because they don't know how to cook!'

'This is true?' asked Kep, a look of amazement on his face.

'Oh yes, it's entirely true,' I answered with a straight face, flabbergasted they didn't understand the joke.

Stella grinned and winked at me, causing a moderate breeze due to the fake eyelashes she's taken to wearing lately.

'Well, we shall have to arrange cooking lessons for them then,' said Sputnik.

'Paaaaah…You can't be serious? I'd like to be there when *that* happens.'

'Maybe we will manage these beautiful creatures better than human beings have.' He looked down his cauliflower nose at me.

'Yes, yes of course, teaching lions how to cook will definitely stop them from becoming extinct.'

Armstrong frowned at me, so I changed the subject. 'Let's go and see the elephants.'

'Esme, we were hoping you could give us extra information about the creatures within the exhibition,' said Sputnik as we walked. 'We recognise your expertise in some things and as such would like to pick with your brain.'

'OK, well I can tell you some stuff about elephants. For instance, when do you think is the best time to feed baby elephants?'

'Well, I'm not sure,' said Sputnik.

'We humans have discovered that the best time to feed baby elephants is when they're hungry.'

'Well of course it is, but what is the exact time?'

Really? I don't know why I bother.

The elephants were soooo beautiful, Mum. I wish you could have seen them too.

'How on earth did you get these here?' I asked, changing the subject.

'Simple. We have further developed a technology which can shrink creatures,' he said. 'You, yourself, will have experienced the shrinking procedure when you first entered the spaceship. This technology has been harnessed and the result is a brand new device called a Minimiser. When pointed at a specific creature, it will reduce it in size to the proportion needed to be transported back to Kratos.'

He paused for effect, a smug look on his face, before continuing, 'Upon delivery to the exhibition the creature is simply placed into its enclosure and reconfigured with another device, a Maximiser. Thereby restoring it to its original proportions.'

'Is that how you've transported all of these creatures back?' asked Stella.

'Not all, just the dangerous ones, and the larger ones like these elephants,' he replied. 'The domestic creatures, such as the dog and the cat, are easy to handle. They shrink alongside our students when they return to the spaceship.'

'A dog? You have a dog? Here?' I asked. 'I've always wanted a dog, but we couldn't have one because my mum is allergic to them.'

'Yes, yes, have you not seen it yet?' asked Sputnik.

'No, there wasn't one here last time. Where is it? In the farmyard zone?'

'No, it's in a new area, which we've been working on for some time now. It's recently been completed. Would you like to come and see it?' he said.

'Would I like to come and see it? Would the wind like to blow? Of course I would. Is everyone else OK with this?' I asked.

'Affirmative.' said Stella, who, along with Kep, had got caught up in my excitement and was just as enthusiastic to see this new addition to the exhibition.

'Come on then, let's go,' said Sputnik with the first sign of energy I'd seen in him since we'd met. We walked across to the enclosure I'd seen being constructed the last time we visited. It was covered in curtains though.

'Why is it concealed with extensive textiles?' Stella asked.

'This is a special exhibit which we are opening later this week. You've come at just the right time,' Sputnik said, giving an uncomfortable-looking Armstrong a greasy grin.

'What's going into it?' asked Kep.

'That's a state secret.'

'Why's he acting so weird?' I asked Stella as we walked around the enclosure, trying to peer inside.

'I am not aware of any strange behaviour.'

Then something awful happened. I mean awful as in, on a whole new, titanic level of awful.

All a bit tricky, chocolate biccy. ☹

Love,

Esme

xxxx

24

27 February

What do you mean, they've already left?

'The dog is just around here, in the new enclosure,' Sputnik said, leading us around the side. He opened the blue door using fingerprint recognition and motioned for us to enter.

There in the middle of a small room was the cutest, most adorable and furriest puppy I've *ever* seen. What's more, he loved me as much as I loved him, moving away from the others whenever they stroked him, bouncing all over me.

His name's Monty, and I think he's a spaniel. He's brown and white, with big floppy ears and the most beautiful eyes. He's everything I've ever wanted and more.

I felt so sorry for him though, Mum, being stuck here in outer space, away from his family. He might be well looked after, but it's not the same…

Looking up from puppy-playing level, I saw Armstrong deep in conversation with Sputnik by the door, nodding his head, tapping his chin.

'Esme, I'm going to take Kep and Stella over to Insectopia,' Armstrong said, finally dragging himself away. 'I know how much you hate insects, would you like to stay here and play with the puppy for a while?' I couldn't think of anything I'd rather do more, so obviously agreed.

Which was my first mistake.

'OK, Stella, say goodbye to Esme,' said Armstrong.

'I will observe you once again shortly,' she said, before following Kep out of the room. Which just left me and Sputnik.

'You can take your spacesuit off if you like,' he said. 'Once this door's locked the enclosure is sealed, so the atmosphere is completely safe for you.'

'Well, I'll be leaving soon, so I won't bother,' I said. As tempting as it was, it seemed like a waste of precious minutes away from playtime with the pup.

'I'll bring you some food soon,' he said as he edged towards the door.

Random. Do I look undernourished now?

'I've never knowingly turned food down, so go for it!'

'If you want to explore the enclosure a little more just push the door there,' he said, pointing at the purple door in the corner. 'There's a light switch on the right as you enter. If you need anything, just press the button to alert me,' he continued, motioning towards a small panel on the wall by the mystery door.

He left, shutting the external door tightly. I played with the pup for seventeen minutes and twenty-two seconds before it occurred to me that Stella hadn't come back for me.

Neither had Sputnik with the promised food.

I think Monty was hungry by this stage too, as he looked like he was about to lick the pattern off his food bowl. I pressed the button on the wall, hoping someone would come and take me back to my Kratos family, not to mention feed Monty.

'Have you been through the purple door yet?' said Sputnik through the intercom.

'No, I've been playing with Monty. Can you please come and feed him and let me out? I want to see Stella. I don't want them to leave without me,' I was trying to stay positive, squishing down a rising panic.

'Yes, I'm going to bring some food in. For both of you in fact,' replied Sputnik's disembodied voice calmly. 'However, I'm afraid your friends have already left.'

'What do you mean *they've already left?*' My stomach sunk faster than a lift at a department store sale. 'I... I don't understand, why would they leave without me?' I picked up the pup and hugged him close.

'They had no choice. The decision was made some time ago, I'm afraid. In fact, even before you arrived on Kratos. We've just been waiting for the right time.'

'But—'

'Why don't you take a look behind the purple door. I'm sure you'll appreciate the effort we've made to make you as comfortable as possible.'

'What are you talking about?' I knew I had to walk through the door to find out for myself, but was terrified at what I might find. The penny had started to drop, but I actually needed to see it to believe it.

I was right, but it was much, much worse than I'd imagined.

Bleary-eyed, gonna hide. ☹

Love you to bits,

Esme

xxxx

25

27 February

The galaxies suck

As I walked through the purple door I was stunned into silence. I'd entered into the enormous enclosure I'd seen being built on my last visit. The one behind the curtains.

Inside was an exact replica of my bedroom on Earth.

Oh.

My.

Days.

It was like they'd transported my entire room to Kratos. All my furniture was there, and was in the same position as my bedroom back home.

My daisy rug was there, complete with spaghetti sauce stains. My bed – with my favourite duvet cover – pushed up against the back wall, which was covered in my wallpaper. There was even a ten centimetre strip of wallpaper ripped off next to my bed, from when Isaac last played his '*let's wreck my older sister's bedroom*' game.

My eyes darted across the room, from left to right,

153

then back again. A mix of fear and wonder washed over me, replaced by astonishment when I clocked the photo of Gran on the wonky bookshelf. It was all too much. I couldn't stop myself from crying. I was properly homesick already. Seeing this made everything so much worse.

'Do you like your new home, Esme?' a voice I recognized asked through the intercom, startling me out of my distress. Mrs Wobbleton!

'I don't understand, why am I here?' I asked. 'Can you help me, Mrs Wobbleton? Please? Does Stella and her family know where I am? Do they know what's happening?'

'There are a large number of people who have invested heavily in this particular enclosure. We are members of Hamsana, a group who are committed to finding solutions to Kratos' problems. Members bear the mark – the Hamsana Oculus.'

So that explains the tattoos I've been seeing on people. They're part of some not-so-secret society. Who else was involved?

'And in answer to your questions,' she continued, 'Armstrong and Luna are fully aware you are installed in this exhibition. You are a rare specimen. The prize exhibit, in fact – the human alien. We want to share the experience of knowing you with everyone.'

'Surely it would've been easier to have given me my own reality TV show? *Esme Takes Kratos*. Or *Keeping Up With Esme*,' I said, in disbelief. 'You can't keep me in this small space forever.'

I couldn't believe Stella's family would go along with this evil plan. But then I remembered the whispered conversations, how Luna had become all tearful and huggy. The pieces of the puzzle were coming together.

'It is essential to maintain a close watch on you – being on TV would not allow the close observation this enclosure permits. Plus, the many thousands of people who are unable to travel to Earth will enjoy seeing a real human, close up.'

'That's the worst reason ever,' I protested. 'It's not only cruel, but against my human rights!'

'You forget, you're not on Earth now. You have no 'human' rights. That is an inalienable fact.' I could almost see her smirking.

'You will be doing Kratos a great service. Our society highly esteems Earth, we emulate many of your ways. Countless people will pay to see you, and the money raised will be ploughed straight back into research.'

'Why did you let me live with Stella's family if you intended to imprison me here all along.'

'It has been interesting observing you integrate, but it was never our intention to allow you to live amongst the Kratons. Unfortunately we had no choice but to collect you before the exhibition was ready. Missions to Earth can only take place at specific times of the year. The galaxies decided your arrival date.'

'The galaxies suck.'

'If we hadn't brought you here at the time of your

arrival, it would have necessitated waiting for the galaxies to realign before we could collect you,' she carried on. 'They can be unpredictable. Mission trips typically get less than one week's notice. I, for one, was impatient to see you installed here at the earliest possible date.'

What kind of alien thinks it's OK to take a perfectly normal – *OK,* normal-*ish* – girl away from her friends and family and lock her up in an enclosure?

Away from her natural habitat. Existing only for the pleasure of people willing to pay money to come and see her. I was sitting on the bed, staring at everything around me, wondering what on Kratos I was going to do, when Mrs Wobbleton interrupted my thoughts again.

'I'm sorry you're unhappy, but I'm sure given time you'll come to terms with it. You may eventually thank us. Your species is in danger of becoming extinct because of the mess you've made of your planet.'

'What are you talking about?'

'War, global warming, poverty. You name it, Planet Earth is doing it. You humans base your level of happiness on your possessions. Your level of joy is directly linked to how many things you can claim to own. Your favourite word is 'mine'. The more you say this word, the happier you become. Such a shallow way to live.'

'If Earth's so bad, why do you keep copying so much of what we do?'

'Your planet has many good qualities. We will

extract these and use them for our purposes,' she replied. 'And the global warming which is taking place, whilst alarming for your species, is very interesting to us. We are experiencing global freezing here on Kratos. It will be catastrophic if we don't find ways to halt the process.

'We are looking to Earth to teach us how to warm our planet up. You've done *such* an excellent job of overheating yours.'

'I don't think it's *that* bad.'

'It makes no difference to me what you think,' she snapped. 'Now I'd like to ask you some questions.'

'I'm not answering any more of your stupid questions. As of now, this human is officially off limits to anything you might say, do or ask.'

She left me alone after that. I cannot believe I've got myself into this situation.

We got into an argument about zoos, didn't we Mum? But when you said they were cruel and unnatural, I thought you were just trying to impress Protest Pete. Now I totally get where you're coming from. It's just a shame I had to actually experience it myself to understand.

Harsh. ☹

After Sputnik delivered food, I took my suit off and wandered around the room. It was lovely to be in normal clothes for a change, but imprisonment is too high a price to pay for the privilege.

I picked up Gran's photo and started crying again. I don't think I'll ever stop missing her. Sitting on the bed, I instinctively looked under it for a secret stash of biscuits and sweets. Of course the space was completely empty. Sad as I was, I couldn't help feeling triumphant.

See, you didn't get everything right!

I kept worrying about Stella finding out. I was pretty sure she'd be devastated when she realised what had happened. Not to mention angry with her parents.

Lying back on my bed, I curled up on my side with Gran's photo snuggled close to my chest. That's when it struck me. I'd been so distressed before, I'd not had time to consider. How did they know what my bedroom was like? How did they get this photo of Gran? Who's the only person from this planet to have been in my room?

Stella!

She *must* have been involved in all of this. Otherwise they wouldn't have known how to put my bedroom together so accurately? And she *had* to have stolen Gran's photo. The final piece of the jigsaw dropped into place. My bad day had just got a whole lot worse.

Betrayed by the first person I've trusted in years, I thought as I munched down on a sandwich, trying to take away the taste of captivity.

I swear if I ever see Stella or her rotten parents again I'll make them wish they'd never met me.

I wish I'd never left home, Mum, I've been so stupid!   And now I'm stuck here.

Thank goodness I have my kTab on me. At least I can keep the blog going.

Feeling low, cookie dough. ☹
Love you and miss you,
Esme
xxxx

26

28 February

A special shade of mean

The next day I had a visitor.

Stella.

It didn't turn out quite the way I expected.

She'd somehow managed to get permission to come into my enclosure because she was apparently 'inconsolable' when she found out what had happened to me. At least that's what she told me. I didn't notice her at first as I was busy playing with Monty.

She just stood and cried.

And cried.

And cried.

'What are you doing here?' My face was as red and furious as my hair. 'I know it was you who set me up. I thought you were my friend! Traitor…'

'Esme, you must perceive that my honesty is not without doubt. I had no comprehension of this strategy,' she said, a pleading look in her eyes. 'I have corresponded with the head of Hamsana to demand your immediate liberation.'

'Oh yeah? Then tell me, what was your mission to

160

Earth? I know every single one of you on the STAR Programme is instructed to bring something back with them. What was yours?'

She stood staring at me.

'Everyone else brought something back, but you brought nothing, right? But you did, *didn't* you?' She studied her feet, clearly distressed.

'It bothered me that everyone was congratulating you on your successful mission. I asked you, but you kept avoiding the question. I couldn't see for the life of me what you'd brought back. But of course, I wouldn't have seen... *would I? Because I was your mission, wasn't I?*' I shouted, making her wince.

'Affirmative... you were, but my mission was simply to make good connections with you, then transport you to Kratos. Her bottom lip quivered. 'I knew nothing of this proposal to incarcerate you.'

'I don't believe you,' I snapped.

'My information was that you would unite with my family upon arrival, thereafter residing with us. This is my solemn oath to you. If I had any perception of these inexcusable schemes, my agreement to participate would never have occurred.'

'Whether you knew or not, you still lied to me.' The truth is I wasn't sure what to believe. 'By not telling me your mission, you left out vital information. You *deliberately* misled me into running away with you. If you *did* know this was going to happen, well... that makes you a special shade of mean.'

'I was obeying instructions from Mrs Wobbleton. I was not permitted to notify you. Only my parents and the captain of the spaceship knew. They were ordered to behave in a manner which suggested they had no prior knowledge. My options were severely limited.'

'You stole my Gran's photo from my bedroom!'

'I am aware, and my apologies are exceptionally deep and sincere. My instructions included to remove and convey various personal items and to take a photograph of your bedroom. I had no conception such activities were designed to recreate this.' She swept her arms across the room, pausing for a moment to gauge my reaction.

'I have persuaded my father to assist me in liberating you,' she said. 'Upon realising the full extent of my anguish, he has become preoccupied with bottomless remorse. Similarly, his options were limited. Hamsana made great insistence on multiple occasions for him to comply.'

'All he had to do was say no.'

'This is inordinately complicated, Esme. The STAR Programme is funded by powerful people who belong to Hamsana. My father has subsequently updated me. They have participated in urging him to surrender you into their custody on numerous occasions. He initially declined, however, eventually the pressure became too extreme, therefore he surrendered.'

She looked sincere as she told me this, but still, to be betrayed is a tough one. After one minute, fifteen seconds of silence, I burst into tears, at which she pulled me into a huge hug.

'What am I going to do? I can't stay here like this,' I said, clinging to her.

'Have negative anxiety, my family are employed upon a strategy which will secure your release.'

'Well, can't you work a bit quicker?'

'My father is maximising the connections he has with the associates of Hamsana. If this fails to produce successful outcomes, our actions will transfer to Plan B.'

'What's Plan B?'

'It is not fully formed at this precise instance… but do not fear, there will be a solution to this predicament. We will navigate through this disaster, I promise,' she said, looking like she had the whole planet on her shoulders. 'Kep has responded to your predicament with particular distress. He has an extensive comprehension of the alarm you are experiencing. His familiarity with the consequences of being detained as a hostage is vast.'

She put her hands on my shoulders and looked me in the eye. 'Your liberty will be ensured, have no fear,' she said before leaving me to wallow in my misery.

I sat down with a thump on the bed. What was to become of me? The opening of the *Me, Myself and I* enclosure, starring Yours Truly, is happening tomorrow. Once it's taken place they'll *never* let me leave.

Monty bounced onto the bed and, with a puppy-dog burst of energy, licked my face and nuzzled my neck. I gave him a belly rub, loving his warmth. But even he couldn't cheer me up for long.

The fact is I'm stuck here, Mum.

Nobody cares about me apart from Stella. She says her family want to help but, aside from Kep, I don't trust them.

So there it is.

I'm officially the star attraction in this stupid exhibition. I know I've always craved more attention, but this is taking things way too far.

'Be careful what you wish for, you might just get it.' That was one of Gran's favourite sayings. Boy was she ever right. I didn't realise it would turn out this way. I never would have left if I'd known…

Actually, I never would have left if I'd known how much I was going to miss you all. It's taken me this long to understand that nothing and nobody can replace you.

Give Maisie and Isaac a big cuddle from me please. Tell them I love them.

Alien plots, miss you lots. ☹

Love,

Esme

xxxxx

27

1 March

☆ A natural habitat for the human alien ☆

Arriving ten minutes before the opening ceremony, Sputnik told me what was going to happen. It sounded awful.

It was worse.

At 3 p.m. the crowd entered the room. Sputnik had switched the sound panels on, so I could hear the bustle and excitable chat. I couldn't see anyone though as it was still shrouded by thick curtains.

I was both looking forward to and dreading the 'unveiling'. I wanted to see who was there, but at the same time I knew any privacy I'd enjoyed up to this point would be rudely ripped away from me once those curtains were pulled.

'Ladies and Gentlemen,' began the voice I'd come to loathe, 'it is my great pleasure to welcome you to the Opening Ceremony of the Planet Earth Exhibition. We are delighted to be celebrating this special day with the unveiling of our finest installation at the Planet Earth Exhibition – the human in its natural habitat.'

I could just picture The Wobbleton's razor-sharp smile, head nodding in appreciation at the applause. Her lifetime ambition had finally been achieved. I wondered if any of them would care about what was happening to me.

'I'd like to invite Sputnik to the front to explain the installation in more detail.'

There was silence for twelve seconds before I heard, 'Yes, well… um… a lot of time and effort has been put into creating a natural habitat for the human alien. Her enclosure is cutting above the rest,' he said. 'Our principal STAR student scoured Bournecombe for the right materials. Our exhibition workforce have been labouring around the clock to bring you this magnificent jewel in our collection of all things Earth.'

'How has the human taken to her new environment?' asked someone.

'Why, she's been doing remarkably well. She seems very content with her surroundings,' Sputnik replied. 'The STAR student who collected the human, Stella 12,614, was highly efficient in gathering all manner of data and information for us,' he carried on, little guessing the effect his words were having on me.

'Therefore, we have been able to accurately assemble the human's living space. She has also been provided with an Earth creature she has long desired, but been unable to have due to her mother's damaging immune response. A dog.'

It's called an allergy! And it wasn't your fault we couldn't have one, Mum. You can't help being allergic to dogs. Plus it would have meant one more mouth to feed…

'Yes, we wanted to make it as comfortable as possible for the human, so we invested heavily in her living space,' said Mrs Wobbleton, reclaiming the mic. 'We've even provided books and learning materials to enable her education to continue. Studies have been made of exhibitions of this kind on Earth. They call them zoos. We are anxious to avoid the mistakes some of them make.'

There was a murmur of approval from the crowd.

'There are some of these so-called 'zoos' which house animals in the most appalling conditions. They are cramped and with no familiar habitat. They are neglected, underfed and offered no medication when sick. Some of the creatures show clear signs of distress,' she continued.

'These poor creatures pace or rock backwards and forwards repeatedly, bite their bars and suchlike. Hamsana, whilst fully supporting the Planet Earth Exhibition, will not tolerate any form of cruelty to the creatures we have captured, forced from their natural habitat, away from their families and enclosed in a confined space for the remainder of their natural lives. Indeed, we are committed to providing the best care possible…'

Blah, blah, blah.

'Finally, it gives me great pleasure to introduce you to our special guest this morning. Miss Eclipse Total!'

Everyone went mad with excitement, clapping and whooping. *What was she doing here?*

Then I remembered her chatting to Mrs Wobbleton when I appeared on *The Rodney Swineheart Show*. She must be connected to the whole flippin' thing.

Is no one on this planet a decent alien being?

'Why, thank you for such a wonderful welcome,' said Eclipse in her whispery voice. 'You can't imagine how excited I am to be here today. I must say that when Mrs Wobbleton told me of Hamsana's plan I was initially concerned.'

Finally, here's somebody who does care.

'Then I spoke to several people who have been monitoring Esme since she arrived and they convinced me the right thing to do was to place her into this exhibition,' she continued. 'I just know she'll be happy here. From what I've heard it will be an improvement on her life on Earth, where I understand she was extremely unhappy.'

Stella again!

'Also the research Hamsana is doing will surely benefit generations to come on Kratos…'

I zoned out. In a moment of genius I knew exactly what I could do to spoil their plans. Provided by The Wobbleton herself, it couldn't fail…

In a while, Earth girl style. ☺

Love,

Esme

xxxxx

28

1 March

My public awaits

'It's so thrilling to witness this step forward for the exhibition. With this in mind, I've written a song, which I'd like to perform now.' Finally Eclipse finished speaking… but was now going to 'sing'.

Could this day get any worse?

It was pretty much the worst song I've ever heard. I don't get what they see in her. Surely Kratos must have some talent somewhere?

The lyrics say it all:

We all have a dream
A dream we hold onto for years
This dream that we hold
To stop all the cold
To bring our planet
Back to Earth.

Dreams of a winter
Long since passed
Dreams of a summer
Designed to last.

169

We call on you now
Kratons around the world
Join us as we see it come
True...

Building a better future
For you and for me
And for my family
Building a better
Kratos to come
I'm so happy
I'm home.

We all have a dream
A dream we hold onto for years
This dream that we hold
To stop all the cold
To bring our planet
Back to Earth.

It can only get better
Only get better
Only get better
Now
Hamsana's here
It can only get better
Only get better
Only get better
For you
And me.

Showing us how to live
Showing us how to give
The winter will be totally
Gone for good.

GONE
FOR
GOOOOOOOOOOOOOOOOOOOOOOOD

If I had a sick bucket I would have filled it. Seriously, this is the best this planet has to offer? I was just grateful that I couldn't see her, listening was bad enough.

'And now, without further ado,' Mrs Wobbleton said after the applause had died down, 'Eclipse will unveil the installation.'

This was my big moment…

I started pacing up and down with the most miserable face I could pull out of my facial expressions bag. The curtain fell. There was complete hush for twenty seconds before someone finally said, 'Is this truly what a human habitat looks like?'

'Extraordinary,' said someone near the front.

'She looks distressed,' said another as I sat on the bed, rocking backwards and forwards, a fast river of dribble flowing down my chin.

Out of the corner of my eye I saw Mrs Wobbleton. In her black dress splattered with stars, she looked like my worst nightmare. She was talking furiously to Sputnik, who shrugged his shoulders at whatever she was saying. Her eyes rolled round and round as she turned to look at me, disbelief written across her face. Anger steaming from her ears.

'This is most unusual,' Sputnik said to the audience. 'It is not her usual mode of presentation.'

'We are inclined to believe she may be performing, to provoke sympathy for herself,' said Mrs Wobbleton.

Rumbled.

'Why would she do that?' asked the reporter. 'If she was happy, surely there would be no need to perform.'

Exactly.

With that he whipped out his kTab and started taking photos of me. Not wanting to disappoint, I added more feeling to my 'performance'.

I banged my head against the Plexiglas.

I bit my headboard.

I wailed and groaned.

I rocked backwards and forwards.

I blew bubbles with my spit.

Pretty soon, others were taking photos of me too, complaining loudly about 'the poor human' and saying stuff like 'shocking' and 'disgraceful' and 'shouldn't be allowed'.

Sputnik disappeared, along with The Wobbleton.

I can't begin to tell you how much satisfaction I got out of it, Mum. I'm so much better at this drama stuff than I realised. If I ever get back to Earth I'm going to take it as one of my GCSE's for sure.

I looked up and spotted Armstrong staring at me, a look of sadness on his face, mixed with an expression of admiration. He knew exactly what I was doing and was impressed.

'Esme,' said Mrs Wobbleton through the intercom. 'Stop this nonsense this instant. Failure to do so will result in your food being rationed.'

I must admit I did hesitate for a moment, but nothing – not even food – could stop me.

'Why thank you, Mrs Wobbleton,' I said. 'But as you've no doubt noticed, I have enough on my plate already. Those ideas you gave me will come in very handy indeed.'

I turned to face the security camera in the corner and, with my back to the audience, gave an enormous smile, followed by a wink so sarcastic it could probably have taught Advanced Sarcasm at Wink University.

'Now if you don't mind, my public awaits, and I would hate to disappoint them.' I twirled around, quickly resuming my *I'm deeply distressed, now go tell the planet* performance.

Sputnik came back out and declared the exhibition closed for the day. My first battle won. Now to win the war.

As he was leaving, Armstrong nodded his head and winked at me.

I'll update you as soon as I get any more news. Needless to say, I'm looking forward to annoying my captors again tomorrow.

On that note I'd better go practice my headboard-biting…

Fighting back, Esme attack. ☺
Love,
Esme
xxxxx

29

3-4 March

☆ They may be watching

The people who've visited have tried to make contact with me through the Plexiglas. Sputnik's turned off the sound panels though, leaving me with no option but to rely on my acting skills. I hope they'll go forth and shout out to the whole planet about my suffering.

If I was in a film that was up for an Oscar I would win hands down. Except I really *am* miserable, so technically, I'm not acting.

Loads of people have complained to Sputnik. I've not been able to hear exactly what's been said, but they've been properly shouty, waving their arms around all over the place.

This morning I saw three families talking to him at the same time. The kids were crying and pointing at me.

Result. ☺

Stella came yesterday. Sputnik refused to let her into my enclosure so she just stood outside, crying so much the floor was covered in purple gungy tears and people were slipping up. Someone landed on their bum and had to be carried away on a stretcher, at which point Sputnik declared her a health hazard and sent her home.

Anyway, she came back again today, this time with a note from Mrs Wobbleton giving her permission to come inside. Which was ever so slightly good timing because I've come up with a plan to escape.

'Your lack of presence at home has been decidedly difficult, Esme. How has your experience been?'

'How do you think it's been?'

'I understand Sputnik has provided reading material for you…?'

'Yes he did, and the good news is the books are brilliant.' The truth is I'd forgotten how much I enjoyed reading. I'm usually glued to the TV at home. Now I'm in a position where I have nothing to do I've been practically inhaling them.

'I have unfortunate news for you, Esme. My father has been unable to secure release for you. The maximum important person has recently informed him that his request has been categorically refused.'

'That's OK, don't worry.'

'Clarify, what is occurring here?'

'I'd rather not. Now can we change the subject please?' I scrunched up my eyes, gently shook my head. Thankfully she got the message.

The rest of our time was spent playing cards and then chatting about school. Stella is still getting on well with Obi, blushing a bright shade of blue when I asked after him.

Mars sent me a card with a lovely message in –

Hope I that are you too not unhappy. Miss you we.
She really *does* need to sort out her language, but, as
Gran would say, 'it's the thought that counts'. Except
where Mars is concerned, because no one knows
what her thoughts are and – unless she deals with her
syntax issues – they never will.

Stella got up to leave, so I pulled her in for a hug.
Slipping a letter into her pocket, I whispered, 'Don't
react, they may be watching. I've come up with a
plan. I need to get out of here, and sooner rather than
later.'

I've had a lot of time to think while I've been in
here, Mum, and I've come to a decision. If… I mean,
when I get out of here, I'm coming home.

I think everything is going to be alright.

Things are looking up, buttercup. ☺

Love,

Esme

xxxxx

30

☆ *Tell someone who's bothered, Sputtypants* ☆

The number of visitors has gone down so I've been a bit bored the last few days. I've only seen Stella and her family. Oh, and Sputnik of course. I quite enjoyed performing my display of pain and angst, so my main source of entertainment has been taken away from me.

There's been a major disturbance outside the entrance every day. I can just about see the main door if I stretch my neck far enough, but I can't actually see the protesters. I can hear them though. They sound like a right angry bunch.

I hope they can spell better than you, Mum. ☺

'When are you going to get the message?' I asked Sputnik as he delivered my food this morning. 'There's no point in keeping me here any longer. People are even boycotting your precious exhibition now.'

'You are indeed correct. It does appear rather futile under the circumstances, but circumstances can

178

change,' he said, growling at me. 'You've certainly put on an impressive display. So much so that we are expecting a visit this morning from representatives of the Society for the Treatment, Rights and Observation of Progeny.'

'What are they coming here for?' I asked.

'The people from STROP have, like the rest of the planet, been watching the news.' Spotting my confusion, he continued, 'Yes, you've made the headlines, or rather the protesters have. STROP is a charity that has been established to help children in distress. Despite the fact you are an alien, they are coming to investigate.'

'So I'm getting out of here?' I asked, jumping up from the bed, sending cushions flying.

'This is a very real possibility, but not guaranteed,' he replied, looking at me with distaste. 'It would be such a waste if they demanded your release. The work we put into getting you here, creating this enclosure, will have left and dropped down the drain.'

'Tell someone who's bothered, Sputtypants,' I folded my arms. 'How would you like to be locked up somewhere like this, stared at for 'research' and 'entertainment' purposes?'

My outburst shook him out of his mood. 'I would have thought you'd feel honoured. You're the first human to have ever lived on a planet other than Earth. We've welcomed and embraced you.'

'Welcomed and embraced?' I said in disbelief. 'If this is your idea of being 'welcomed and embraced' then goodness *knows* what your idea of poor

179

treatment is.'

At that moment, a group of five people, one carrying a Dictaphone, the others with clipboards, shuffled up to the front of my enclosure. Sputnik hurried out to stand with them as they observed me.

I thought about doing the usual head-banging, tongue-lolling, dribbling thing, but somehow it didn't feel right. So I just sat down in front of them and stared at them, pleading with my eyes for them to get me out of there.

One minute, thirty-two seconds later I was weeping. Not crying, but big, fat teardrops, each one carrying a tiny piece of pain slowly down my cheeks. The agony of the last week was unleashed in this one moment. I wasn't acting.

The one with the Dictaphone turned to Sputnik and whispered something, turning him a bright shade of blue. Nodding his head several times, Sputnik backed off, racing towards the entrance.

I scrawled across a piece of paper. *Please get me out of here.*

A few scribbles later and one of them held up a sheet of paper. *We have every intention of securing your release. Sit tight.*

With a sharp nod, he and the team walked in the same direction as Sputnik.

I expect you can imagine how relieved I was. Well, times that by a thousand and you'll have it about right.

Thirty-five minutes later, Armstrong and Stella stood in front of my enclosure with the biggest grins.

I raised my eyebrows questioningly. She nodded, her jaw stretched to near breaking point, her antennae bouncing around like they were dad-dancing at a wedding. I began to cry again, but with relief this time.

Sputnik bustled up. Shooting them a look of irritation, he made ready to open the door to the enclosure.

'Esme, you must put your spacesuit on,' he said. 'You are being released into Armstrong's custody immediately.'

'Yes!' I turned towards Stella and punched the air. After dressing as quickly as humanly possible, I grabbed Monty. 'Come on, we're getting out of this dump.'

'No, you are not permitted to take the puppy anywhere. He has been bred for the Planet Earth Exhibition. He belongs to us, therefore he is not permitted to leave.'

'But what will happen to him?' I asked, feeling close to tears again.

'That is not your concern. Once you've left this building you will never see him again.'

Picking Monty up, I hugged him tightly. He snuffled my neck and licked my face. There was nothing for it, I had to leave him if I wanted to be free. But that didn't stop my heart from breaking into tiny pieces all over again.

'Esme, I need you to understand that Luna and I had no part in the decision to keep you here,' said Armstrong as we walked along the corridor towards freedom. 'The people within Hamsana are very powerful, some even have government positions. I was threatened with the loss of my job and then my home. I am ashamed of the outcome of my decision.'

'I understand you were put in a difficult situation. I might have done the same if I'd been you. I love my family very much too.'

'But you said—,' began Stella.

'I know what I said, but feelings change. I've realised how much my family means to me,' I said, stopping by the entrance door. 'Let's talk later, my public awaits.'

Outside the exhibition we were blinded by photographers who'd gathered to capture the moment of my release. Armstrong hurried us into the Jetcar. Stella sat with me on the back seat, her three right arms around me.

I know I should have been ecstatically happy, Mum, but leaving Monty behind was so hard. All I could hear was his whimpering as I walked away.

Why does life have to be so difficult?

Still, it *was* good to be free. Armstrong switched on the TV when we got in, so we could watch the latest news report. I knew the protesters had been outside the exhibition, I just hadn't realised how many!

Led by Stella, Armstrong and Luna, the protesters had been standing outside for days. The news report showed around 150 of them waving banners and shouting things like *'Save Esme, let her out'* and *'Free the human alien'.*

The TV presenter was interviewing the head of

the Social Care Keepers, Mr Snotgrass. *'In what has become known as 'Esmegate', we understand you were personally involved in the decision to free the human alien from the Planet Earth Exhibition?'* the reporter asked, talking to Snottypants' dad but beaming confidently into the camera. He obviously thought he was the best thing since sliced garlic bread. *'Can you tell the public what influenced your decision, sir?'*

'Well, it was not a difficult decision to make,' he said. *'If you'd ever met the human child you would have done the same. Why, she is intelligent and articulate, more so than many of our own children. To even consider locking her away in that exhibition was monstrous. Monstrous, I tell you.'*

I'm 'intelligent and articulate'. Did you hear that, Mum?

Amazing. ☺

Having already turned away from him, the reporter faced the camera, flashing his sparkling smile again, *'You heard it here first, on Kratos Broadcasting Corporation. Stay tuned for an update on the reported sightings of alien activity, east of the Plain of Vinteron. Plus the latest report from KASA indicating that there may still be life on Hyperion! All this and more on your favourite TV station, KBC.'*

Luna and Armstrong started talking about my future. As far as I can see, I don't have one. At least not here. I'm leaving, and this lot are going to help me.

'I want to go back to my own planet,' I said, to no

one in particular.

'What did you say?' asked Armstrong.

'I said, I want to go home,' I repeated, louder this time.

'I think you'll find that once the fuss has died down you can continue as normal,' said Luna gently. 'I've already spoken to Mrs Wobbleton and she's said that, providing you allow them to continue with their observations, you may go back to school next week.'

'So everyone's just going to forget about the whole "capturing me and locking me in an exhibition" thing and make like it didn't happen,' I yelled, rolling my eyes. 'Well, *you* might be able to forget but *I* can't.'

I looked around the room. Everyone was clearly shocked by my outburst.

'Look it's not just that. I've realised I miss *my* family. I felt like this even before I was locked up. There's so much I've enjoyed about living on Kratos, but this isn't where I belong. I need to go home, to be with my own species.'

'*Shooting stars*, Esme, what on Kratos are you thinking?' asked Armstrong, prompting Luna to raise her eyebrows and give a sigh of exasperation. 'You can't leave here, they'd never allow it.'

'Well then I'll just have to find a way to escape,' I said, sounding way more confident than I felt.

'Father, we can surely provide her with assistance?' asked Stella.

'Yes, we should help her return to her family,' said Kep. 'I remember only too well how it feels to be apart from my family, many miles from home. Home – a place your feet may leave but your heart will always be.'

'This is entirely different,' said Armstrong.

'In what manner is it different?' asked Stella.

'Unlike Kep, Esme has a warm and loving home. We are very fond of you and will always look after you. You will be provided with the best of everything. This is my solemn promise to you.'

Luna went across to him, gently touching his shoulder.

They looked at me hopefully. I felt so bad; after all, they'd helped me escape the exhibition. But there was no way I was staying.

'I'm so grateful to you for helping me escape, but I need to go home,' I said, my voice trembling. 'I miss my mum, even her nagging. I miss my little brother and sister, despite them driving me nuts. I need your help. Please?'

'It is clear Esme has a deep and understandable necessity to be reunited with her family,' said Stella.

'It is wrong to keep her here against her wishes,' said Kep, his look hugging me with sympathy.

'I have an idea that may work,' I said. 'But I need your help.'

'I think we need to let her go, Armstrong,' said Luna.

Armstrong looked around the room, realising he was outnumbered. 'But it would be practically impossible, even if I agreed to it,' he said, shaking his head.

'*Practically* impossible, but not *completely*,' I

said. By the time I'd finished outlining my plan everyone was smiling.

'You know it might just work,' said Armstrong.

'Naturally. If Esme has concocted the strategy, I am certain of its success,' said Stella.

I'll let you know when I'm back on Planet Earth. In the meantime, don't worry about me, I'll be perfectly fine. It's a good plan. Not a lot can go wrong. Unless of course I get caught escaping or the spaceship crashes or some other bad stuff happens.

Obi came over and everyone played games all evening. He'd refused to come and see me in the exhibition out of principle, but had been part of the protest group campaigning for my release. It's nice to have such good friends. But that's all they are. Friends.

You, Maisie and Isaac are my family.

Coming back, union jack. ☺

Love,

Esme

xxxxx

31

10 March

☆ *Inordinately satisfied with me* ☆

Stella's been busy putting my plan into action. She was so excited by the time she got home from school today, her antennae were thrashing around again. As usual it was not a good look.

'Wait, calm down,' I said. 'Just tell me what happened.'

'Well,' she said, catching her breath, 'you ascertained correctly, the stars are aligned to permit a return STAR mission to Earth and there is a solitary position remaining. Mrs Wobbleton asked Mars but she said, 'Sorry, am I, nervous I and miss my want don't I to birthday 18th brother's.'

Stella's grin was now as wide as a humongous grin that's spent four years at Grin University and passed with a distinction.

'Sooooooo… then… youoooo…?'

'Immediately volunteered!'

'She agreed?' I had fingers and everything else crossed.

'Affirmative.' Clapping all six of her hands together with excitement. 'I depart next week. Currently she is inordinately satisfied with me.'

'Brilliant!' I said, jumping up and high fiving her right hand. The one nearest the ground.

The first part of my escape plan is a success. Stella is scheduled to go back down to Earth on a STAR mission.

The second part is likely to be trickier – getting me onto the spaceship without being noticed. But that's where Kep is going to come in…

Over the moon, see you soon. ☺

Love,

Esme

xxxxx

32

17 March

It's been lovely borrowing you

It was so much easier for Dorothy. I wish I had a pair of ruby slippers I could just click together and, in an instant, be home. It's taken me a lot longer than her to realise 'there's no place like home', but now I have I can't wait to see you all again!

I've been so nervous I've hardly slept this week. It's hard to leave them. Apart from the imprisonment episode, they've been like family to me.

'Come on, Esme,' said Luna, giving me a hug, 'it's time to get you home, where you belong.' I hugged her back. I knew I wouldn't have the opportunity once we got to the STAR Centre. If anyone saw us carrying on like this they'd be suspicious.

'Are you sure you want to do it?' I asked Stella again on the journey. 'If you get caught you'll get into big trouble.'

'Your value is such that I am delighted to assist you, Esme Tickle,' she said, her eyes brimming with tears. 'I regret making an agreement to transport you to Kratos. I am exceedingly pleased to have the opportunity to rectify the situation. You are the most significant friend I have ever possessed.'

Armstrong nodded in agreement as he was driving. Luna gave me a sad smile, her eyes glistening, 'Yes, we will miss you and your peculiar Earth ways. It's been lovely borrowing you. But it's time to return to your real family.'

By now *I* was crying. 'Thank you for everything. I'll miss you so much,' I said. 'Armstrong, I love the way you put your family first, above everyone and everything else. And Luna, you have so much hair on your chin now, Hairy Harrison's looks threadbare in comparison.'

'See, it was worth all that effort, wasn't it?' she said. I don't think I could have paid her a bigger compliment.

'Anything worth having is worth fighting for,' said Kep.

Why does life have to be so complicated? You find some aliens you really like and then you have to go and leave them. But it's true what Gran used to say, 'home is where the heart is.'

Walking into the STAR Centre I quickly spotted Mrs Wobbleton in front of the spaceship, being interviewed by several school reporters. How was I going to get past her? Hopefully Kep would do *exactly* what I told him to.

Some younger students were being shown around.

'This is a newer model of the Vader Spaceship Cruiser. The earlier models were symmetrically uneven, thus causing issues with balance upon launch and landing,' said the guide.

'It is large at this point, only decreasing in size once it reaches the Earth's atmosphere, whereupon it shrinks to 43.4 cm, which of course enables us to land on Earth without detection.'

'What's 'detection'?'

'It means without being seen by humans,' the guide said. 'Now, where was I…? Oh yes… The technology we have developed enables our students to leave the spaceship, where they gradually reconfigure and become larger again, taking on the appearance of the indigenous species – the human.'

There was a collective 'ooh' from the students.

It sounded properly scary, but I'd done the journey before and survived, so I figured I'd be OK doing it in reverse.

Before long Stella came out of the building, kitted up ready to go and looking really pleased with herself. She stood at the bottom of the stairs leading into the spaceship, posing up a storm for a photographer from the school magazine. It was wonderful to see her surrounded by some of her new friends, who'd arrived to see her off.

This was it.

I wandered over as casually as I could, for all the universe looking like I was just a friend saying goodbye. Suddenly an enormous scream ripped through the air, followed by a commotion from the viewing tower.

Everybody turned to look. Kep's antennae were

well and truly caught in the entrance door. There were pints of fake blue blood spilling everywhere. At least two people had fainted.

Mrs Wobbleton raced across, leaving the way open for me.

I turned for one last look at Armstrong and Luna, before dashing into the spaceship as fast as my legs could carry me. The stowaway capsule was exactly how I remembered it. I nearly yanked the door off its hinges as I scrambled to get in without being noticed.

Four minutes, twenty-two seconds passed in deadly silence. Then I heard a voice I'd hoped to never hear again.

'I know you're in there, Esme 1,' said Mrs Wobbleton. That voice sent chills down my spine.

Rumbled.

Deciding to stay put, I prayed that she'd find a more interesting recipient of her attention and disappear. Or faint.

Or something like that.

No.

Such.

Luck.

'A clever idea, sneaking on board while I was distracted, but these new ships have extra-sensitive motion sensors. They record everything, including unwanted stowaways.' She opened the door. 'Get out this instant!' she hissed, irritation hitching a lift along with her voice. 'And as for you, madam,' she said, turning to Stella, 'you have a lot of explaining to do.'

Grabbing us both, she herded us through the

crowd towards the main building, her grey and white dress finning behind her. Once inside, she shoved us into a small, windowless room.

'Whose idea was this?' she demanded, a snarl slashed across her jaws.

'Stella had nothing to do with it!' I gave her my best filthy look.

'This is correct?'

I silently begged Stella not to admit to anything. I know it's wrong to lie, Mum, but if they found out she would never be allowed to take part in any more STAR missions Which meant I'd *never* have a chance at getting home.

'Negative. I had zero comprehension of this conspiracy,' she said. 'If I had awareness I would have advised Esme to remain on Kratos. The danger involved in returning to Earth is extreme.'

'Quite right too,' said a voice behind us.

Sputnik! That was all I needed.

'You are telling the truth, Stella?' asked Mrs Wobbleton.

She looked the picture of innocence as she nodded.

'Very well then, you shall be permitted to rejoin the mission,' she said. 'Sputnik, watch the human while I return Stella to the spaceship.' With Stella in tow, The Wobbleton sashayed back to the spaceship.

Meanwhile I was stuck with Sputnik.

Great.

Except it was. Great, I mean.

Really great in fact.

Heading back, midnight snack. ☺

Love,
Esme
xxxx
xxxx

33

☆

17 March

☆Operation I'm a human, get me out of here ☆

☆

'Esme, I'd like to help you escape from Kratos,' Sputnik said.

I looked up at him. He sounded like he meant it.

'Why would *you* want to do *that*?'

'It made my heart to shatter into a thousand pieces when I saw how unhappy you became.'

'Really?' I asked, astonished at this sudden turn of events.

'No, of course not! I have no choice but to help!'

'Why?' I asked.

'Because I suggested it might be a good idea,' said a familiar voice.

Armstrong followed his voice into the room, with Kep wandering in closely behind, fake blood splattered down his shirt. Sputnik scowled at both of them. I looked from one to the other, trying to figure out this new turn of events and failing miserably.

'Say 'bubbles', Sputnik,' said Kep.

'Why?'

'Just say it.'

'Bubbles,' said Sputnik reluctantly.

'There, see,' said Kep. 'No one can say the word 'bubbles' and sound angry.' And it's true. Although Sputnik was still glaring, he didn't look nearly as angry as before.

'Can somebody tell me what is going on here?' I pleaded. 'And can we *please* quit with the bubbles chat. The Wobbleton will be back quicker than I can say "ooh look, there's ten Greater Spotted Froids".'

'I "persuaded" Sputnik to help you escape if the first plan didn't succeed. He had no choice,' said Armstrong. 'Kep here was helping Rodney Swineheart's team research a TV special on the work of Hamsana, when he uncovered some rather unsavoury facts about Sputnik's activities outside of exhibition hours.' He glared back at Sputnik.

'He's been using the equipment to sneak creatures out, selling them to private collectors who pay millions of Orbits for them.'

'Yes, and I was doing very well, thank you, until your brother started poking his nose in,' said Sputnik. 'You made a promise that if I stopped the trade and helped Esme escape, you wouldn't tell anyone. Will you keep your end of the bargain?'

'Naturally, I am an honourable man. Now tell me what you're going to do to ensure my silence.'

'Integrity is doing the right thing when nobody is watching,' Kep chipped in.

'Can everybody *please* stop talking and just get on with it,' I said, desperate to get *Operation I'm a*

196

Human, Get Me Out of Here moving along as swiftly as possible.

'Yes, I have something up my arms which will guarantee you are home by the end of the day,' Sputnik said. I felt hope rising again.

He whipped out two objects from his pockets. 'These are examples of our latest technology – a Minimiser and Maximiser.'

'No way are you using them on me!'

'I have used the Minimiser already today, have no fear it is perfectly safe. Watch I will demonstrate,' he said, taking out a tiny creature from his pocket. He placed it on the table, aimed the Maximiser at it and, in a wag of a dog's tail, Monty appeared. A normal-sized version, in his very own custom-designed spacesuit.

'Monty!'

'Yes, part of the deal was that you could take him back with you,' said Armstrong. 'I saw how broken-hearted you became after leaving him behind.'

'Oh, thank you!!'

'You will be fine, Esme. Allow Sputnik to use these gadgets. I wouldn't suggest it if I thought you were in any danger.'

'Come. Now. We must make big with the haste,' said Sputnik. 'Over to the middle of the room, please.' I followed his instructions and held Monty tight as he unlocked the Minimiser.

'Remember, Esme, winning takes talent. To repeat takes character,' said Kep, over Sputnik's shoulder. I nodded nervously, waiting and wishing I could just get the next few hours over and done with.

'Once I've used the Minimiser, I will place you in the pack I've prepared for your transport. When you're safely inside Armstrong will carry the pack to the spaceship and place it in Stella's hands.

'He will give her a sheet of paper with full instructions on how to use the Maximiser. She will then simply restore you to your normal size in your hiding place once you've taken off.'

He aimed the Minimiser first at Monty, and then me. Within 0.24 nanoseconds I was as small as a cherry tomato.

He scooped us up and popped us into the pack, strapping us in. 'I wish I could say it's been nice knowing you,' he said, sighing as he zipped the pack up.

'The feeling's mutual,' I said, but stopped when I realised my words most likely sounded like a squeak.

The next three minutes and twelve seconds were a bit of a blur. I could feel gentle movement and muffled voices. For a moment I was worried he might be trying to trick me and, rather than help me, was going to keep me secretly locked away for eternity.

Finally I heard Stella's voice. It was muffled but I'd recognise it anywhere. Even though I couldn't make out what was being said her voice got squeakier, so I guessed he'd told her about us. We were carried a little further before I heard a door opened, and a jolt as the pack was set down.

I'm not going to lie, I was properly nervous, but knowing I was coming home, and having Monty helped a lot.

Five minutes and thirty-four seconds later the spaceship began juddering like a washing machine on a fast spin cycle. Lift off!

Before I had time to even think about what I was going to say to you, there was a rap on the door and the pack was lifted again.

Stella opened the zip, gently took us out and zapped us back to our normal size with the Maximiser. It felt like every atom in my body was heated up… expanded… twisted… until I was back to my normal size.

'Phew, glad that's over. How long until we land?!' I stretched every part of my body, doing my best to get rid of the weird tingling running around it.

'Have much patience. Merely one million light years separates us from Earth. Settle back into your capsule. I have activated the oxygen, so you may safely remove your spacesuit once I have sealed the capsule. We will arrive very soon.'

She was right – once out of my suit I barely had time to scratch my nose before the spaceship juddered to a halt. I waited until I could hear Stella and the others stirring before making my move.

Peering cautiously around the open door, I could see straight through to the ground outside.

English soil. Then I heard the most amazing sound I've ever heard – the hooting of an owl. My stomach did a whole bunch of cartwheels, somersaults and double back-flips.

Or something like that.

I really was home!!!
Back on the block, party frock. ☺
Love,
Esme
xxxx
xxxx

34

You're kidding me, right?

I could see others moving down the stairs and knew that, as they walked further away from the ship, they were reconfiguring, taking on human form again. Fortunately for me, I didn't have to worry about the 'human form' bit, it was the 'reconfiguring' I was worried about.

Still, I thought, if I failed to rise to the challenge of becoming my normal size, there was always the Maximiser Stella had stashed in her pocket.

It took all my effort not to race straight out the door. I needed wait, to let the others get off first. Boy was it good to breathe natural air again.

The distance between me and the door was 2.46 metres, which meant I needed four seconds to get to it and race down the stairs. Once the general movement had stopped, I decided to go for it. I popped my head out again to check the coast was clear, then, with Monty tucked under my arm, ran!

Which was just as well because, at that precise

moment, the stairs were starting to rise and the door was seven seconds away from shutting completely. I could hear the engine revving up again.

So near yet so far.

Running as fast as a bullet from a gun, I just managed to hit the stairs in time to leap down before they were completely drawn up. Landing with a crash on the damp ground, I jumped up, grasping Monty even more tightly as I scrambled towards the cover of the trees.

He tried to wrestle out of my arms but, worried I'd lose him, I held on even tighter – sssshhhhing him for good measure.

Hiding behind an oak tree, I breathed a sigh of relief. The tree seemed to approve of its surroundings, and I was in total agreement. It was a pretty special place.

The simple pleasure of standing on solid, earthy ground overwhelmed me. I inhaled the scent of the grass and damp logs, heard the owl hoot again.

Lush.

Gran used to tell me that no one knew what they had until it was gone. I've learned that on so many levels since I left.

Suddenly from out of the darkness I heard a rustle, followed by a small voice. 'Esme.' Phew, it was just Stella.

'I'm over here,' I walked across, my feet making gratifyingly scrunchy sounds on fallen branches. She was at the edge of the clearing – the only place the moon hangs out when it visits these woods. The spaceship was gone, so we stepped into the light.

She'd gone back to being the Stella I'd first met, the human version. An antenna caught my attention, sticking out from under her hat like it was checking the wood out. I pulled her over and repositioned it.

'I don't know how to go home,' I said, looking sheepishly at my feet.

'Have no trepidation, I will sho–'

'No, I mean… well… I know the way, I just don't know how my mum's going to react when I walk in the door. I'm scared, I don't have a clue what to say to her.'

'For what specific reason would she retain excessive displeasure with you?' She was smiling, her eyebrows arched.

'Oh well, I guess it's not much. I only ran away from home for two months, left Planet Earth without permission, to go and live with a bunch of aliens. Put myself in harm's way again and again before risking my life to come back,' I said, my eyebrows mirroring Stella's. 'Yep, you're right, why would she be cross with me?'

'Your comprehension is confused as I have not provided the complete factual elements of this situation.'

I wished she would stop grinning.

'Time progresses with exceptional speed on Kratos. You have been absent for two months on my planet, however Earth's time is much slower. You have been absent for—'

I grabbed her wrist and stared at her watch. My

eyes nearly popped out of my head. It showed the date to be…

Wednesday 16 January.

10.14 p.m.

'You're kidding me, right?'

'No, your absence has amounted to one hour, fourteen minutes, Earth time.'

'But… but I wrote the blog… You encouraged me, you said it would help my mum 'come to terms' with me leaving,' I spluttered, swinging backwards and forwards between relief and disbelief.

'In truth, I sincerely believed maintaining an online chronicle would facilitate *your* emotional wellbeing. I had negative notions that one day you might return to Earth. I certainly did not contemplate your mother would access it.'

'Oh my days, so all this time I thought my mum would be worrying about me, she didn't have a clue,' I said, more to myself than Stella.

She looked at me with concern in her eyes. Reaching out, she gently placed her hand on my arm. 'It is perfectly acceptable, however, for it indicates there has been no emotional distress experienced by your mother. Therefore you may surely reappear with little difficulty, for her life has not been altered.'

'I know, but I wrote so much. I wanted her to understand how I felt about things,' I said. 'I wanted her to know why I was unhappy with things the way they were at home. And that now I understand her a bit more.'

'You must surely dialogue with her. This will

enhance your relationship,' she said, matter-of-factly, shrugging her shoulders.

'Talk? My mum barely has time to brush her teeth, never mind sit down to talk.' It felt hopeless. I really wanted to come back home and start a whole new relationship with you, Mum. I couldn't see how that could happen if you didn't understand what I'd been through.

'Alternatively, you could present these chronicles to her. Permit her to inspect and engage with them?'

'She doesn't like reading much, but maybe if I told her it was about me and what I'd been up to she might be interested.'

'It is of greater importance that you improve your relationship, regardless of your mother's inspection of your chronicles. I am inordinately gratified that you have achieved something positive from your experience on Kratos.' She hooked her, now singular, right arm through my left one. 'Come, let us commence the walk to your habitat.'

Fine and dandy, cotton candy. ☺

Love,

Esme

xxxxx

xxxxx

35

☆ *I've not been myself lately* ☆

We walked through Barrow Wood, chatting away like old times. Snottypants was waiting for us at the end of Daisy Way.

'Hello, girls, it's good to see you again.' She actually sounded like she meant it. 'It's getting very late, and you've have had quite enough adventure for one day. You can fill me in on the details tomorrow at lunchtime.'

She turned to Stella. 'You should be tucked up in bed, so it is essential we go to the house. Esme, you must come and visit. It's where all the Kratons stay when they're visiting Bournecombe.'

Err, no thanks, I think I've had enough of being around aliens for a while.

'Thank you for helping so much today. I couldn't have made it without you,' I said to Stella.

'I will observe you tomorrow at school.'

'Yes, see you then!'

I ran along the road with the enthusiasm of an

energetic tortoise that's just won a race against an asthmatic hare. Monty sniffed every tree and bush like he'd never seen one before. Which, of course, he hadn't.

But I wasn't running because I was trying to keep up with him. I was excited to be home. I could barely contain myself.

All the things I'd taken for granted before were slapping me in the face with their fabulousness. By the time I reached my house I was sprinting as if my life depended on it.

As usual there was plenty going on when I arrived home. From the front door I could hear Maisie and Isaac fighting upstairs. I used to hate hearing them, but now I couldn't get enough. I soaked up the sounds for twenty-one seconds, before tying Monty to a bush in the garden and pushing the front door open.

I found you in the front room, sitting on the sofa quietly crying. There was a box of pink tissues next to you, and a few scrunched up in your hands. I stood and watched you for thirty-five seconds.

'Mum?' I said, finally breaking my silence.

'Esme?' you looked up sharply, before jumping off the sofa and coming towards me. 'Where've you been? You know you're not allowed to go out after dark! I've been so worried about you, and then I saw you'd taken some of your clothes, and, well... after what 'appened today I thought you'd run away. Come 'ere love,' she said, pulling me into the most wonderful embrace of my entire life.

Mum, you have literally no idea...

207

'I'm really sorry, I shouldn't have left without trying to talk to you,' I mumbled, before pulling away. 'It's just that you've always got your mates here, or some bloke. It doesn't feel like I belong here sometimes.'

'What are you talking about, love? You're my number one daughter. I love you. Just 'cos I don't tell you every day, doesn't mean I don't feel it.'

'But all you seem to have time for is your mates, or whatever boyfriend you've got.'

'I know love. It's not been easy since your Gran died. I've not been myself lately. Abbie was in the living room earlier... you know, when you came 'ome and got upset with me and Pete. After 'e left, she told me a few 'ome truths.

'She said I don't look out for you enough, that I need to give you more time now that you're about to become a teenager. We 'ad a row and I kicked 'er out. But then when I found you missing earlier, I was thinking about it all, and... well... she's right, isn't she?'

'But Mum, I know how—'

'No, we'll have no excuses. I feel like I've stepped out of a fog tonight and seen things the way they really are for the first time in months. Things are gonna change around 'ere. I don't ever want you thinking you're not important.'

'I love you Mum, and I've missed you so much. But I don't want you to completely change. That would be *too* weird.'

'I know, and me and Pete... well, we do 'ave a

special bond, we'll still be doing the animal rights thing. Now I know you don't agree with it, but–'

'Mum, you couldn't be further from the truth. I may even join you one day, just as long as it's not outside my school again!'

You stared at me then, as if I'd turned into some kind of alien.

The yapping from the garden reminded me. 'Oh, I've got a surprise for you, give me a minute,' I said, before racing out to rescue Monty from the garden.

'Where'd 'e come from? You need to take 'im out quickly! The last time I was this close to a dog I 'ad a nasty rash for over a week.'

'It's OK, Mum, he's specially bred. Non-allergenic, like those pillows you can buy. The person I got him from told me we can keep him, so can we? Please?'

'Seriously? I've always wanted one But I'm not sure we can keep 'im. 'E'll take a lot of looking after and they cost money to feed, you know. But, oh my,' bending down to stroke his silky coat, 'you are an 'andsome boy, aren't you?'

I made us the happiest cup of tea of our lives, before Maisie and Isaac came running down to join us. Once they heard Monty's yapping there was no stopping them. I grabbed them both and pulled them into my arms. They gave me weirdest looks, but let me squish them anyway.

The rest of the evening passed in a haze of noise, laughter and barking. It's wonderful to be home.

I'd left to put some space between me and my family, but then realised it was the opposite of what

I needed.

And it was the wrong kind of space.

Signing off for now, but I may write some more posts, so come back for an update.

Home to stay, forever and a day.☺

Esme

xxxxx

xxxxx

17 March

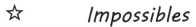

Impossibles

Dear Reader,

If you've got this far I expect you're doubting my story. That's understandable. If someone had told me some of this stuff I'd have suggested they needed to seek the services of a medical professional. For a very long time.

Impossible, right? Maybe.

But I'll tell you what's impossible…

It's me and my mum talking regularly. Laughing at the little things in life, enjoying each other's company.

She's started to open up about my dad, which has helped me to make sense of a few things. Apparently he walked out when she was four months pregnant. She doesn't know where he is. It's hurtful, but I'd rather know than be left in the dark, always wondering.

She's not seeing Protest Pete any more. She couldn't get him to change his bossy ways towards me, my brother and sister. So she dumped him. She's told me she's 'having a break from men' for a while.

Result. ☺

When I come in from school I don't go straight to my room like I used to. I spend time with my family. I often make Mum and her mates a cup of tea and help Maisie with her homework. Sometimes I even cook spaghetti bolognese. A better version of the one I made for Armstrong and Luna, naturally.

We've joined an organisation which campaigns against animals being kept in poor conditions. I've adopted a tiger at an amazing conservation park, which treats its animals well, giving them lots of outdoor space and a proper diet. It's set up to rescue animals rather than just catch them and keep them in captivity just to entertain people.

Impossible is Mum, Maisie, Isaac and me going out for a meal together at the Thai Tanic, during one of their 'buy-one-get-one-free' lunchtime specials.

Just the four of us, nobody else tagging along. All having top banter. Mum shouting, 'Come on you lot, we'll be late!' Me yelling back, 'Well, if you'd started shouting at us earlier, we wouldn't be late, would we?' And getting away with it.

Impossible is me spending time with Maisie and enjoying it. This girl is seriously clever. Like when she's playing with dolls on the floor and I say to her, 'Which doll can I be?' she says, 'You can be the one who does the dishes,' on the evening it's her turn to wash up. I love the way she sees the world. I think she may be a writer one day.

212

Impossible is babysitting my barmy little brother. Settling down to watch a cartoon on the sofa, with him snuggled up to me, is my idea of heaven these days. I love, love, love his Isaacisms, which are becoming more and more ambitious every day. He's still fixated on his bum though. (What is it with boys and their bums?!)

I was helping Maisie with her reading the other day and he ran past, letting out a huge fart, which stopped him in his tracks. He turned to us and said, completely straight-faced, 'Oops sorry, that was my bum saying thanks for the food!', before running off screaming with laughter.

Nuts. ☺

Impossible is actually enjoying school again. Becky Morgan stays out of my face now. I don't think she's ever lived down 'Foodgate'. And my teachers are gobsmacked at my sudden enthusiasm for learning. Especially the geography teacher, who gave me the top grade for this term's 'Global Warming' project. She commended me for my 'excellent research, alongside my passionate and articulate call to action'.

Brilliant. ☺

Impossible is Dylan Grant, yes THE Delicious Dylan, deciding to hang out with me. He says that I've changed somehow. Apparently I'm 'more chilled'. We chatted about Mum's animal rights shenanigans and he says he admires her for standing up for what she believes in.

I had no idea that Dylan's mum was a single-par-

ent. She's allergic to dogs too, so I sometimes take Monty over to his house. We're thinking of starting up a dog-walking business, to maybe earn some money to help our mums with bills and stuff.

I've tried to tell Mum about my adventures on Kratos, but she keeps telling me I just have an 'over-active imagination'.

I wrote the last four blog posts from home on my kTab. I wanted to finish the story because I'm hoping one day she'll read it. She says she knows something's happened, loves the new me and can't get over the change. But she can't get her head around the idea that I lived in outer space for two months.

Understandable I guess.

Impossible is me not taking my family for granted. Loving them just the way they are, not hankering after what other families have got. Sure my little brother and sister can still be annoying, but that's family, right? I still wish I had a proper dad around. And nothing can change the fact that Gran is gone for good, but it is what it is.

We may not look like what some people think is a normal family – and we're definitely not perfect – but they're mine and I love them.

Who gets to decide my family isn't normal any-way? Who says we should have dessert after the main course? Isaac likes to drink the milk straight from his cereal bowl. Who decided that's the wrong way to do it? I've always tried to stop Maisie colouring outside of the lines, but why shouldn't she?

I don't have the answers to these questions, but

Stella said it's the questions that are important. I've come to the conclusion that some things are different, but it doesn't necessarily make them bad. It just makes them… different.

*None of us gets to choose our family, or its shape and size. But whatever our family looks like, we've just got to count our blessings and appreciate what we **have** got.*

Monty and my kTab aren't the only things I brought back from Kratos. I think it's fair to say that the most important things can't be seen.

I've learned that love is a special thing. It can be unexpected, creep up on you when you're not looking and slap you round the face.

But it can also be hidden, lying underneath the surface. If you look at a lemon, you just see the outside of the fruit. You wouldn't know there was all that juice inside unless you squeezed it. The love I have for my family was there all along, under the surface. I just needed Kratos to squeeze it out of me. Right now, I feel like I have enough lemon juice to set up a lemonade factory AND a chain of lemonade shops across the country.

I was sad to leave Stella's family behind. It was fun for a while, but I'd wrapped them around me like a coat in winter. But it was never my coat to wear in the first place. And, like any coat, it had to come off eventually, because the seasons change.

I sometimes go and sit at the top of Barrow Hill on my own, just to stare at the night sky. I always count my lucky stars that I'm home. Who knows, I may go back one day. But for now I'm making the most of every precious moment with my family here.

It's true what Gran used to say, 'friends and family come in all shapes and sizes'. And, I should add, sometimes even species.

I'll leave you with some wise words from a very special friend of mine:

Be nice.

The end.

Peace out, brussel sprout. ☺

Love Esme,

#galaxygirl

x

ACKNOWLEDGMENTS

To my University of Winchester MA Writing for Children peers, who were a great bunch to study alongside. A special thanks to Claire Symington, who has read and critiqued this book at its various stages with tremendous patience. You've been a wonderful source of encouragement from the off. Thank you for loving Esme as much as I do!

To my lecturers at Winchester University: Vanessa Harbour, Judy Waite and especially Judith Heneghan, who helped me to shape #galaxygirl in its early stages. Thank you for the kindness, encouragement and support during a very tricky period. It helped to keep me going, both with the MA and the writing.

Thanks to Emma Pass, who helped me wade through the mayhem that my plotting had become. Also to Becca Allen, whose copy editing skills helped to make the book much more readable.

To the members of SCWBI: I've learned so much from you over the last couple of years. Thank you.

Thanks to Helene, who encouraged me to step out and follow my dream, prior to my joining the MA. Also Ania, Jula, Kirstie, Jen, Elspeth, Chris, Sharon and Amanda for your faith in my ability.

Thanks to my friends for your unwavering support: Heather, Kathy, Lizzie, Emma and Laura. Thanks for listening, offering ideas and endless encouragement.

To Nicky, Ben, Sam and Max, thank you for providing accommodation during the dark winter nights, allowing me to stay after late Uni sessions.

A special thanks is needed for my work family at Crestwood Community School, Eastleigh. Your support, kindness and belief in me over the previous couple of years has been immense. Carole, Jess, Juliet, Krista, Loretta, Nicky and Steve. Thank you.

Also thanks to my LPO work family, in the UK and France, especially Tim and Alison. Thanks for tolerating my obsession with writing, and for still smiling at me when I haven't changed the topic of conversation for hours at a time.

Thanks also to my family for your support. My two sisters Louise and Natalie, whose belief in me goes above and beyond the call of sisterly duty. My brother Nick and sister-in-law Rachel, who are a great encouragement. My mum, thank you for encouraging me to read from a very early age and for providing all the books I gobbled up as a child.

To my nan, who is sadly not here to read this. I based Esme's gran on her, and just like the fictional one, my nan was a rock during my childhood. Like Esme, I'll never stop missing her...

My three girls, Sophie, Amie and Chloe, and my wonderful son-in-law, Davy, for tolerating my long absences and strange witterings.

I got there in the end.

ABOUT THE AUTHOR

Bev has been a secondary school teacher, saleswoman, waitress, wages clerk, youth worker and holiday park children's and youth programme manager. She has scuba dived the Barrier Reef, lived in the Namibian bush, worked for a charity in Thailand and paddled in the sea at Bournemouth.

Having single-parented her three daughters, she's been ferociously playing catch up with this writing lark. She recently completed a Masters in Writing for Children at Winchester University.

LETTER FROM BEV

First of all I would like to say a huge thanks for investing time and money into buying and reading *#galaxygirl*. It means such a lot!

In my teaching career I've come across so many 'Esme's', each of whom has made an impact on me. I, therefore, started writing the book with a clear picture of who Esme was at the beginning and who I wanted her to be at the end. I wasn't sure how I was going to get her there, and it took a whole lot of plotting, re-plotting and rehashing, until I was happy.

There is a lot of humour in the book, and a number of themes that are close to my heart. However, I hope that the key theme of the importance of family, whatever its shape or size, shines through. If you relate to Esme, please do find someone you can trust and talk to them. Perhaps a teacher at school or a relative. You will find there is support for you, especially if you are helping to care for one of your parents.

Whatever you do, don't run away. And *especially* don't run away to outer space!

If you are interested in animal rights and would like to investigate further, then visit www.wwf.org. uk. The World Wildlife Fund explains how you can get involved in protecting many species.

I hope that you enjoyed the book! If you did, please could you write a review, either on Amazon or Goodreads, or wherever else you bought the book online. I'd love to hear what you think, and it would be wonderful to help others find my book.

If you would like find out more, please go to my website:

www.bevsmithbooks.com

I can also be found on social media:

https://www.facebook.com/bevbooks/

https://twitter.com/BevSmith612

PS Keep your eye out for the next book in the #galaxygirl series, to be published in 2019.

Lightning Source UK Ltd.
Milton Keynes UK
UKHW041028071219
354907UK00002B/179/P